ISBN: 978-0-9969699-3-2

Dodge City is a wicked little town. Indeed, its character is so clearly and egregiously bad that one might conclude, were the evidence in these later times positive of its possibility, that it was marked for special providential punishment.

(Excerpt from editorial letter, circa January 1878)
Washington Evening Star
Washington D.C.

Revel
Knox
Seven Times from Hell

by Michael Shank

Chapter 1

The thin mountain air squeezed his lungs, but there was no time for rest – they were as close as they'd ever been and he had to move quickly.

Bullets hissed past his head as he moved to the edge of the rock. Revel Knox peered down the steep descent at a river in the valley's basin. Another bullet whizzed by his ear.

"No choice," he thought to himself as he jumped. The eight-and-a-half-year-old American Paint, a horse he called Willow and loved dearly, lay dead behin him.

Thought's raced through Revel's mind as he prepared to make impact on the steep downward slope of broken shale, thorn-bushes and tall pines. Time seemed to slow as he fell through the air.

"Had to be a Henry rifle," he thought. *"They were at least a hundred steps out - Jack must have been aiming at my head!"*

The bullet from the Henry long-rifle had dropped a few feet, due to the distance of the shot. It passed through Revel's calf muscle as he sat in his saddle, entering his horse's side. Willow dropped on the spot.

Time caught when Revel smashed into the slope. His boots sunk through rock and mud, causing his body to topple forward into a roll. Pain shot through his skull as his face hit the rocks. Shards of shale cut through the palms of his hands, embedding themselves deep into skin and muscle as he tried desperately to stop the roll of his body down the steep incline.

The intensity of the July sun blinded him as he slid uncontrollably down the mountain side. Shots continued to ring out.

"Get control!" Revel screamed at himself in his mind as his body continued a high-speed fall down the steep slope.

He recognized that familiar taste of copper as blood filled his mouth. One boot teemed with blood from the gunshot wound. The other boot, the one with the hole in the sole, became impacted with mud and small stones.

Pain erupted at the right side of his neck as a second round tore through his trapezius muscle.

"Hit again!" Revel thought as his panic level continued to elevate.

Revel's body slammed to an abrupt stop into the bank of the valley's river edge. He could hear them coming – the four men who had been pursuing him for the past eleven weeks, now sliding down the mountain-side after him.

"Kill him," one of his pursuers yelled and cursed.

Revel quickly felt for his guns. One holster empty, but the other still held his 1867 Cooper double-action, 4-inch-barreled revolver.

He had loved short-barreled guns since childhood, as he'd seen a lot of men die trying to draw long Colt's from their holsters. Revel quickly learned that long-pistols hindered a fast draw, creating the mantra in his young mind, "*Long pistols cause an early grave.*"

Revel was also relieved to find the broken-handled knife still tied to his leg. It was a knife his grandfather had crafted for him many years before.

He struggled in the mud of the river bank as his mind screamed, "*Get up! Move and live!*"

Through extreme exertion and self-discipline, Revel forced himself to his knees. His head spun out of control and he smelled the stench of his own sweat. He spit a mouthful of blood into the fast flowing waters in front of him.

Revel looked down at his left leg. Blood poured from the wound. He was about to vomit when another bullet exploded a small stone next to his hand. He jerked away instinctively while fighting the feeling that the world was spinning around him.

Revel could hear the men shouting curse words and threats as they worked their way down the slope behind. They were getting closer and would be on top of him in a matter of seconds. Gunfire continued to erupt through the canyon.

Revel, now on his feet, stammered as he looked down river. "*A waterfall?*" Another bullet hissed as it passed close to his ear. "*Out of time. Die here or take the chance…*"

With his last bit of strength, Revel dove forward into the fast water of the river. Adrenaline coursed through his veins from the shock of the cold water and the raging current pulled him down into the depths of the river.

His injured, bleeding body hammered against bedrock, scraped over brush and sped toward the falls as he fought desperately to reach the surface for a breath of air.

"Ah," Revel gasped, inhaling as he broke the surface of the water. He could see the fall's edge… now only a few yards away.

The current yanked his body under again and then… weightlessness.

"I've been a bad man," Revel thought as he went over the brink.

His body hit the water at the bottom of the falls and the world went black…

Chapter 2

Jack Singleton squatted at the edge of the river.

"Whatchu got, Jack?" Everett Pegram asked.

"More blood. There's blood next to this print," Jack said giving reply to Everett. "He's hit, but there's no way to know if it's a mortal wound," Jack admitted.

"We'll get him, Jack. We're gettin' close–"

"Shut your mouth!" Jack ordered.

Jack stood up and turned toward his group of men gathering at the river's edge.

"A man such as this is as cunning as a serpent, and he continues to reveal a unique inner strength – something not possessed by my most current companions." Jack's words were penetrating.

"Boss, you sayin we ain't as smart as–"

"I said shut your mouth, Mr. Pegram," Singleton spoke as he stepped toward his man. "You speak again and the bullet housed within my Colt will be found exiting your spineless back."

"But boss, I just–"

"I said *shut your mouth*," Jack screamed and cursed as he produced his colt revolver at lightning speed and now had it positioned an inch below Everett's left eye, pressing the barrel into his upper cheek.

"Do you acknowledge the precise recognition and understanding of my sentiment, Mr. Pegram?" Jack's question required an immediate and appropriate response.

Everett Pegram's eyes went wild as he stood frozen in place. His lips trembled, "Yes, Mr. Singleton. I understand."

Jack put his meaty thumb on the hammer of the Colt and un-cocked the gun, but did not remove it from Pegram's cheekbone.

"We'll make domestic accommodations for the evening at this spot, gentlemen," he said to the group without moving his gun from Pegram's face. "And we will search for Knox's body on the morrow's first light. Understood?"

Everett Pegram's body began to shake. The other men scurried off to make camp, assuring Jack Singleton that they did, indeed, understand his instructions.

"Mr. Pegram," Jack said as he pulled the gun away from Pegram's face and holstered the weapon, "Help the men." Pegram almost fell backward as he scrambled away from Jack.

Jack Singleton, a forty-nine-year-old ex-US Marshal, was the leader of the cadre. He was a weatherworn man who had outlived two wives: his first wife succumbed to Tuberculosis, and his second died giving birth to their first child. The baby was stillborn.

Jack was also a descendant of wealth and had been educated in the best eastern schools. He had decided, after graduation, to become a US Marshal. It was a decision his wealthy family resented. Jack simply didn't suffer the Elitists, nor did he possess the political aspirations his parents had so desired for his future.

Jack moved to central Missouri to seek an appointment toward his first four-year term as a Federal Marshal where he would serve the district of Jefferson City.

He had, many years before, been a man with a powerfully magnetic personality. His intelligence and chiseled good looks would have taken him to the White House; however, he despised the duplicity of politics and felt that he could better serve behind a badge.

The years of pursuing those who represented evil had, regrettably, taken their toll on Jack. His waxed, perfectly trimmed handle-bar mustache was still in magnificent shape, but his body was beginning to show the wear and tear of the roads he had taken throughout his life.

His joints ached each time a storm front moved into the region. The cigarettes had also given him a chronic cough, and he seemed "winded" from any physical exertion.

Jack's chosen career had also been riddled with struggles and challenges. His life had been one of living on the back of a horse, moving from one straw-camp to another, recruiting and training men of low stature, in an effort to capture the country's most wanted fugitives.

On the other hand, his experiences developed Jack into one of the country's best trackers.

Revel Knox, the fugitive that had murdered two innocent men and injured a third, had become the motivation of Jack's obsession. One of the two men Revel murdered happened to be a man named Bristol… Jack Singleton's brother.

When the US Marshal Service appointed a much younger man to pursue Revel Knox, it proved to be the breaking point for Jack. He tendered his resignation the following morning, relinquishing twenty-four years of service: six terms as an honorable US Marshal.

As Jack threw his resignation onto the USMS's desk, he mentally vowed to turn his back on anyone or anything that represented the law.

He now made his own laws, and the vengeance he sought was working its power on his heart. He, day by day, grew more bitter… and meaner.

Jack and his band of low-life recruits started their pursuit of Revel Knox in Jefferson City, MO. They followed him west by northwest all the way to the Missouri River at the edge of Kansas territory.

Revel's tracks, at Kansas, took them north up the Missouri, all the way to up to the southern edge of North Dakota, some 650 miles from Jefferson City.

They had only been this close to Revel one other time, and that was a few miles north of Medicine Creek, South Dakota.

Jack and his crew, after pushing through an "all-nighter," had found hot embers in a camp-fire that Revel had slept next to just a few hours earlier.

Revel had made the mistake of spitting out his chewing tobacco at the edge of the fire. It was a unique Kentucky leaf twist tobacco soaked in Molasses… the only kind Revel chewed.

Jack had picked it up, smelled it, then put it in his mouth.

"That's disgusting, Jack," said one of his men.

"It is Revel's," he said with a sideways grin, ignoring the comment. That grin motivated his men to push their horses harder, because Jack Singleton never smiled.

Revel's trail turned west at the southern boundary of the North Dakota Territory, crossing the smallest gap he could find in the wide Missouri River. His trail tacked west all the way to the base of the hills at the edge of Wyoming, and then turned due south.

They had pursued Revel to this spot: a location just a few miles south of a newly established settlement named Fort Collins in the Colorado Territory.

"What is it, Mr. Cullum?" Jack asked without turning around. Jack had a creepy "sixth" sense… you could never sneak up on the man.

"Mr. Singleton," Otis Cullum took off his hat. "If we find Knox's body – I'm sorry sir, *when* we find Knox's body on the morrow, the men respectfully request to be made aware of your intentions, sir."

"Knox isn't dead yet," Singleton replied. It was about 9:00pm and Jack was back at the river's edge, studying his prey.

"You, uh… sir, you don't think he's dead?" Cullum asked with a sense of fear.

Singleton stood and turned toward Cullum. He hadn't removed his pistols for the night, which made his men uncomfortable.

"Knox will be dead only when I verify his lifeless body," Jack responded.

"I understand, sir," Otis Cullum said as a whipped pup, quickly retreating to the safety of his friends and the camp fire.

"Fools," Jack said under his breath. "The whole lot of them!"

He walked back to camp, concentrating on Revel Knox. Once in camp he went to his saddlebag positioned on the ground next to the others. Jack found what he was looking for… a flask. He took a drink from the flask and swallowed quickly, trying to ignore the back-burn in his throat.

"*Revel Knox,*" he thought, "*I'm coming for you.*"

Chapter 3

Revel was on his back, unconscious. Horrible dreams combined with excruciating pain made sleep almost impossible.

He opened his eyes and saw a small opening of light in the ceiling above him, but the area around him was pitch-black. A small amount of wood-smoke from the fire at his side filled the darkness.

"Am I in Hell?" Fear swept over him.

Blinding light! For a brief moment a burst of light illumined the space, but then it was gone. Revel clinched his teeth in an effort to control his fear.

He jumped as a soft hand touched his arm. "Hey, what is going on here?" He shouted and cursed. "Who are you? Where am I–"

"*Yee a wana chocto en su saw n nee*!" The delicate voice of a woman spoke from the darkness.

"*Oh, no! Indians!*" thought Revel.

"I don't understand. What are you saying–"

"What is your name?" the voice inquired. She spoke in perfect English with a slight hint of an eastern accent.

"Must be two women here. An Indian and a white woman," Revel's mind scrambled for something rational.

The darkness, smoke, fear, and the strange voices overwhelmed Revel's mind. Tears formed in the corners of his eyes as he laid back, no longer able to hold himself up. Intense pain randomly exploded through various parts of his body.

It was bodily pain that exceeded anything he had experienced in his past. He reached for his pistols… nothing. His skinning knife was also missing.

"You're in a safe place," the woman said from the darkness.

"Where are my clothes? I've got to have my clothes," Revel demanded.

"All of your belongings are here with you," she assured him.

Revel took deep, heavy breaths as a small glimmer of relief calmed his fears. He examined his body with his hands, trying to assess the damage: left calf wrapped in tight cloth, right shoulder wrapped in a cloth under his arm and across his chest, both hands bandaged, broken ribs, cuts all over himself, and pleasant smelling oils seemed to cover his entire body.

"I need a drink," he managed to say.

"Of course," the woman replied from the dark. He instantly felt her warm hands pull his head into an upward position, then felt the edge of a bowl at his lips.

The water was cold and refreshing.

"Slow," she encouraged. "Don't gulp."

"Let me down," Revel responded. The large drinks of water caused waves of nausea through his abdomen.

"Rest," said the gentle voice. "Answers will come."

Revel's thoughts raced between bouts of extreme pain and queasiness.

"I wasn't drowned. Who are these people? The key? Where is the key? Indians pulled me from the river? Why are they giving me convalescence? Revel's mind and thoughts were unmanageable.

He felt himself beginning to fade away, then somewhere outside the tent he heard… singing.

The words were foreign, but the melody? Revel knew the familiar tune of Amazing Grace.

Indians singing Amazing Grace? None of this makes sense…

Revel fell into sleep.

Chapter 4

Jefferson City, Missouri, named after Thomas Jefferson, teemed with life. A village situated on the northern edge of the Ozark Plateau, was in the process of completing its build of Lincoln University: a black college. This part of the country enjoyed and embraced the Emancipation Proclamation, and the community rejoiced in the nation's progress of freedom for all races.

The Village, previously called Lohman's Landing, was now scarcely inhabited by its original occupants: Osage Indians.

German immigrants filled the out-skirts of Jefferson City, creating vineyards throughout the hillsides. Residents had started calling the area, "The Missouri Rhinelands" due to the hundreds of vineyards.

Arthur Ignatius Meade looked through the French window of his opulent Main Street law office watching the progress of Jefferson City. He sipped

Brandy from a heavy crystal glass and drew a puff from a fine cigar.

At forty-five years old, Arthur was beyond his prime.   He was portly and out of shape, but Arthur had the look of success.

The oak plaque positioned at the center of his desk read, "A.I. Meade, Attorney at Law." He spun the cigar counter-clockwise in his lips, tasting the sweet flavor of the tobacco.

It was a July day, mid-morning, and his thoughts haunted him. The Brandy solved nothing, but it numbed his nerves and gave him the false impression that he was invincible… a feeling he coveted.

"Mr. Meade," his secretary spoke through his office's partially opened doorway.

"Yes?" He replied without turning.

"We have word of Mr. Revel Knox."

Meade turned quickly toward his secretary.

She stepped into his office and closed the door.

"A Western Union telegram addressed to you came early this morning–"

"Read it to me, Ms. Townsend," said Arthur as he sat down in the large leather chair behind his desk.

She stepped closer to his desk and read aloud:

```
Revel Knox found just south
of Fort Collins, Colorado
Territory, stop.  Knox body
believed to be injured in
volley of gunfire, stop.

Traversing search area at
present time, stop.  Knox
possibly dead, stop.  Body
believed to be detained in
river, stop.  Hostiles in
area, stop.

Shall convey status at next
determination, stop. Wire
check owed to myself and team
to this location, a.s.a.p.,
stop.
Jack Singleton
```

"Give me the telegram, Ms. Townsend?"

"Absolutely, sir," she said as she handed the paper to Meade and quickly exited his office.

Meade leaned back in his chair and re-read the telegram.

"*Singleton, find that dead body*," thought Arthur, "*or **your** body will end up in a river.*"

Chapter 5

"Boss, he ain't in this river!" Dill hollered from downstream. Dill Oakley was the oldest member of Jack's party, and Oakley perceived himself to be the wisest of the group. Jack waited as Oakley approached.

"Jack, he ain't in this river."

"Mr. Oakley, do you *not* think we've searched far enough downstream?" Singleton looked up at Oakley.

"Yeah. Eight miles down and back. We've searched every bar, eddy, and strainer in this river. He ain't here–"

"And, Mr. Oakley," Jack interrupted as he stood from a squat. "Is it your opinion that we should abandon the search?"

"We're the best tracking team in a five state area and this tomfoolery–"

The sound of the explosion roared through the canyon. Oakley's body fell against the rocks of the river's edge. Smoke emerged from the end of Jack's Colt revolver.

"Mr. Oakley," Jack said to the dead body that lay before him, "Your thinking is poisoned." Singleton put his boot against the head of Oakley's body.

"You," he continued his mock eulogy, "Are a man that has allowed your past successes to poison your existing thoughts.

"You, Mr. Oakley, are a disgusting man who has used the mask of righteousness to hide your own corruption. Mr. Oakley, as God declared in Numbers 32:23, your sins have found you out."

Jack reloaded the empty chamber and slid the revolver into the holster. He thought of his past with Dill. Dill Oakley carried a Bible. He spoke often of God and the need of salvation; however, Dill took advantage of every opportunity to obtain wealth. He never hesitated at an opportunity for "ill-gotten" gain.

Dill's double-minded ways had always disgusted Jack. Oakley was a man who would praise you to your face, then speak evil of you behind your back.

And Dill had a reputation. Jefferson City was full of people who had been taken advantage of by Dill Oakley. Widows that Dill had offered to "help" were later found to be forced to live with their relatives after Dill had forced them out of their homes.

Dill's children were showered with extravagant gifts, but then ostracized if they didn't obey his every command.

"Boss, would you like us to bury him?" asked one of his three men.

"Leave him," Singleton said casually. "All of God's creatures need to eat." Jack walked up-river, along the water's edge. "I'm just sorry that God's creatures will not have a better meal," he said under his breath.

"Get together," Jack raised his voice and the remaining men ran to his side.

"If Revel Knox's body is not to be found in this river, he is still alive," Jack said to his cadre. "The question in my mind that festers forth as puss from a wound is…" Jack paused as he scanned the tree line across the river, "Where did he egress from the water?"

Jack eyed his crew. Every one of them were wet, filthy, hungry, and exhausted.

"And," he continued, "In which direction did he escape?" Jack's voice escalated to the verge of insanity.

"Indians might have got him, boss," said Adel Bohanan. Adel was twenty-three years old and was wise for his age. He kept to himself and answered only at the most imperative of moments. His quiet demeanor was in stark contrast to his ability to inflict violence in a moment's notice.

"Mr. Bohanan," Jack turned to him. "Are you giving voice to your opinion that Knox is dead or alive?"

"Yes, Mr. Singleton. I believe that Knox is still alive, and the most probable outcome is that the aggressives have captured him. Maybe traded him or killed him. Or they could have wanted a trophy scalp."

Jack Singleton was impressed. The young man had mettle and demonstrated a distinct ability to express his thoughts without an agenda of self-preservation.

"Mr. Bohanan, I must agree with your assessment… sir." They had never heard Singleton call any man "sir."

"Get back to the falls. If Mr. Bohanan's idea has merit, we'll find evidence of an extraction point!"

Chapter 6

A heavy Indian woman broke through the tent flap. She stoked the fire then began a thorough examination of Revel's wounds.

"Easy!" Revel hollered out, but his protests were unsuccessful. The woman pulled off the soiled bandages and applied oils to Revel's wounds with rapid efficiency. She applied new bandages and left as quickly as she had entered.

The following days were a blur of uncomfortable sleep, pain, and the constant nursing routine applied to his body by a host of Indian women.

Toward the end of his second week in camp Revel jerked from sleep by a nightmare. Sunlight peered through the opening at the top of the teepee. He could hear an abundance of activity through the teepee's walls of buffalo skins, and struggled as he crawled to the opening.

When Revel pulled the flap open, shock filled his system–

"Dozens… maybe hundreds," he thought to himself as he looked across the camp at the scores of Indians busily engaged in their respective works.

A gaggle of teepees dotted the horizon. There were strands of hides being cured, Indian women and children scattered about, and the comforting smell of venison cooking nearby.

"Where's the white woman?" he screamed out of the teepee. "I need to speak to the white woman," his words trailed off as he came to the edge of passing out. Moments later she appeared through the tent-flap.

"Are you okay?" she asked as she discovered his body at the foot of the opening.

Revel wasn't able to produce a coherent word. She knelt down and put her arm around his chest.

"Let's get you back to bed," her words came out with each tug of Revel's body. "You are not ready to be up and about."

The woman stayed at Revel's side as he slept. Revel woke up about three hours later.

"What's your name," Revel whispered through exhaustion.

"My name is Echoa (ē • *chõ* • *uh*)," she said softly. "It means 'many tongues.' I am what you call a half-breed. My father was an English immigrant, and my mother was Blackfoot. My English name is Millie."

"Millie, I am Revel Knox," he said just before a fit of coughing.

Millie put her hand behind his head and gave him a sip of water. It had been a long time since she had met a white man – especially a man that looked like Revel Knox.

"Slowly, Mr. Knox," she encouraged as he drank from the bowl.

"I am brewing pine-needle tea which should help with–"

"Where are my pants?" Revel interrupted. He remembered the key and panicked.

"Your clothes and things are here with you–"

"Was anything removed from my clothes?" he interrupted again.

"Revel," Millie said gently, "Calm yourself. All is fine. Nothing was removed. Your clothes were cleaned and folded." She pointed toward the south end of the large teepee structure.

Revel looked in the direction of her finger. His clothes were clean and folded neatly in the seat of a primitive, hand-hewn chair.

He was pleasantly surprised when he spotted his grandfather's skinning knife. The blade had been sharpened, as he could see the new edge from where he lay. Someone had, additionally, installed what looked like "bone" into the handle. Furthermore, the handle had been ground down to a smooth, glossy surface.

His Cooper looked like it had been cleaned and oiled, as well.

"Millie, where am I?"

"We are the Shawnokwan Tribe and you are in our camp," She said.

"Shawnokwan? I thought this was Kiowa and Arapaho–"

"Yes," Millie interrupted, "This is the heart of the Kiowa territory. The Arapahos are further south. Shawnokwans have an agreement with the Kiowa people. They give us protection in trade for our willingness to liaison with the whites. We also teach them the English language."

Revel tried to process her words according to his own limited knowledge of the Kiowa tribe.

"Millie, I don't–"

"Shhh," she placed her hand over his mouth. "Worry about nothing but your health for the moment, Mr. Knox."

Her hand smelled like honeysuckle and her voice was as a velvet blanket. His mind reeled with questions, but his primary concerns were the key and Jack Singleton.

"*Singleton won't find me here*," he thought to himself. "*This is a perfect place to hide and recover. And one thing has been established,*" Revel thought to himself, *"They are kind."* "Kind savages?" The two words had never been conjoined in his nomenclature.

Millie woke Revel out of a deep sleep with a bowl of roasted bison and boiled corn. It smelled incredible!

She pulled the tent flap aside and pinned it open, giving him a good look at his surroundings… and her.

The teepee was huge – probably 17 feet from one side to the other. Furs covered the floor of the dwelling and the cleanliness of the space struck Revel.

It was not only clean, but it smelled wonderful… peppermint and sage filled the air. Pine-needle water peddled at a slow boil over the small fire in the center of the space. Hand-woven containers were organized and stacked at the north end.

Millie had sat down next to Revel and folded her legs under herself as Revel's gaze shifted from the interior of the teepee to her face.

"*What a remarkable looking woman,*" he said in his mind. She wore traditional Indian pelts with stitched beading up the arms and the collar of her blouse. Her hair was dark brown, very similar to the color of his own hair and her eyes were a piercing green.

"Mr. Knox," she said.

"Yes, mam," he replied, breaking from his trance.

"Please… won't you eat while we visit one with another?"

"Oh, of course – yes, I'd enjoy your company immensely, Millie."

"Mr. Knox, some of the young men doing reconnaissance have reported that there are a band of men looking for you."

"How many," Revel asked while devouring the bison.

"Five," she replied. "Are you a criminal, Mr. Knox?" Millie said with a mixture of fear and respect.

Revel considered the question as he chewed the meat.

"Mr. Knox, are you a threat to our community?" Milled questioned.

"Mam, as long as those men do not appear at this camp, I am no threat to you or anyone here."

The two sat together and talked. They discussed small portions of their pasts as Revel ate.

"Millie, how long have I been here?" Revel's concern was evident.

"Fourteen nights," she responded.

Fourteen nights? I've got to get moving! Revel thought.

"Mr. Knox, please retire for the evening, but know that I am close by if you need anything throughout the night," she said as she stood from her seated position next to him.

Revel couldn't remember meeting a woman who had such a combination of traits. Millie was kind, respectful, firm, intelligent, and humble. Her presence commanded humility and strength.

"No, mam. I won't bother you any further. Thank you for the meal and kindness," Revel responded.

"Mr. Knox, we will carry you to the river tomorrow. Your wounds need to be washed. God speed to you, Mr. Knox," she said as she stepped through the flap of the teepee.

Her smell lingered in the air and her voice had given him great comfort. He laid back down and wondered:

What was these people's purpose with him? Why were they so... hospitable? What would he owe them when he was made whole? Who was this half-breed who served and comforted him? Was Singleton close by? Would Singleton raid the camp in an effort to find him?

Revel summoned the strength to crawl to his possessions at the southern side of the teepee. He squeezed his hand around his pant-leg feeling for the anomaly – a hidden pocket stitched inside his pants.

Revel hastily unbuttoned the hidden pocket and pushed his fingers to the bottom… he felt the key.

Revel buttoned the pocket back together and scooted back to his bed. Thunder rolled across the sky. A storm-front was moving in and Revel knew his body needed sleep.

He listened to the thunder and swam in his mind. His last thought before unconsciousness… Arthur Meade.

Early morning singing woke Revel. He felt far better *this* morning that he had felt over the past two weeks.

The savages were *singing* again – singing another melody he was familiar with, "*Blest Be the Tie That Binds.*"

Revel stepped out of the tent and saw the large group of Indians sitting on the ground of a large open field next to the camp. They were singing.

He joined the rear of the group of 400 and sat down next to an elderly man. The man smiled at

Revel, then lifted his palms up and down as to say, "Sing with us!"

Revel, not comfortable with singing, just listened. Several more songs were sung and they were all *a cappella*. Revel knew every tune.

A young brave stood among the assembly and began to speak in the Shawnokwan tongue. Revel didn't understand a word of it, but the man's mannerisms and voice inflections were powerful. The young man held a book that looked to be made of an ancient papyrus and hide.

The large group listened intently. There were numerous responses from the audience that seemed to encourage the young Indian man. Women began to weep, but they seemed to weep with joy – not sorrow!

When the young man finished, the entire group stood and sang a song. There was no mistaking the melody – *Just as I Am*.

A bunch of Indians singing Just as I Am! Revel couldn't believe his ears… or his eyes.

Chapter 7

Jack Singleton lay at the edge of the river enjoying the sound of the river. It was late in the evening but his men hadn't gone to sleep. He could hear low talking and whispers coming from around their campfire…

"I say we get out of here," Otis Cullum said to his two associates. Adel Bohanan and Everett Pegram sat "Indian" style next to the fire as they listened. Otis, kneeling on one knee, spoke to his two friends in low tones.

"What? And go where?" Everett questioned Otis through a whisper.

"Let's leave Singleton here and head back to Jeff City," Otis said with conviction. "He's off his rails – he'll keep us out here until he finds Knox, or until he decides to kill the next one of us!"

"You no longer have the stomach for this line of work, Mr. Cullum?" asked Adel Bohanan.

"My stomach is tougher than yours, boy," Cullum responded with anger. "But my stomach is telling me that *this* is a *bad* deal," he finished.

"Boys, stop your bickering. Jack's driving this crew and we listen to him," said Pegram.

Otis Cullum cursed and pulled a drink from his flask. He was feeling the liquid courage.

"It's high time we put an end to this wild-goose-chase," Otis said with as much anger as he could produce while keeping his voice as quiet as possible.

"And I'll tell you boys this," Otis said as he lowered his voice and leaned forward over the campfire toward the two men.

"Jack Singleton can kiss my–"

Otis and the men were interrupted by the sound of a "thump." As soon as they heard the noise, Otis' torso jerked upward into an erect position.

Excruciating pain exploded at the center of Otis' back. He groped toward the source of pain in a panic, not being able to reach the source of the pain.

Pegram and Bohanan jumped up from their comfortable seats around the campfire and backed away as Singleton emerged from the darkness of the forest directly behind Otis Cullum.

Jack walked quickly toward Cullum, focusing on the handle of his knife… sticking out of Otis Cullum's back. Jack reached Cullum in three agile steps, squatted quickly and yanked out the knife.

Otis screamed out in agony and Jack, with lightning speed, pulled Cullum's head backward with his left hand while synchronously slicing Cullum's throat with the knife in his right.

Blood pumped from Otis Cullum's neck. His eyes, wild and bloodshot, grew dim as he slowly slumped forward into the burning campfire. He was dead before his face hit the embers.

Jack Singleton's gaze shifted to the two men standing on the other side of the fire. Everett Pegram and Adel Bohanan were unable to move. Blood dripped from the tip of the blade that Jack held at his right side.

"You boys want to assimilate that advice, be my guest in your cause of abandonment; however, if you decide that staying the course will be most beneficial to your well-being, you are invited to stay and ride with me."

The remaining two men looked at him with a fear they had never known.

"God said choose life or death," Jack said with a voice of a mad man. Everett and Adel could do nothing more than nod their heads in the affirmative.

"And let him burn," Jack said to them as he, ever so slightly, tilted his knife toward Otis Cullum's body.

They looked at Cullum's head. It was faced down and had already begun burning. Everett fought tears and tried to swallow the regurgitation rising from his stomach.

Singleton slowly backed away from the firelight, disappearing back into the darkness of the forest from which he came.

Everett Pegram and Adel Bohanan looked at each other in the light of the flickering campfire.

"We'll get Knox," Pegram said loudly with a curse. He hoped that his boss would hear his enthusiasm.

Adel Bohanan didn't say a word in response, but merely laid down on his bedroll. Everett Pegram followed Adel's lead. Both men faced away from the fire and the burning body of their former associate.

Otis Cullum's body popped and oozed over the hot coals and flames. Everett and Adel lay perfectly still; fighting the sounds and smells of Cullum's burning flesh and praying that sleep would come quickly.

Singleton stood at the boundary of the fire-light just out of sight, watching the last two men of his company fight for sleep.

"*Down to two,*" he thought to himself. "*It'll be good to get rid of the fools,*" Singleton said in his mind.

He cleaned and sheathed his knife. The jagged razor edge had once-again proved its value.

Jack walked quietly down to the river bank, found a large boulder that he could lean against and closed his eyes.

Dawn's light was christened with a scream.

Everett cursed loudly. He was the first awake and was immediately sickened by what he saw at the camp-fire.

Throughout the night Otis' upper body had burned down to bones, leaving a blackened skeleton of the torso, arms, and skull.

However, everything below Cullum's waistline remained in tack. His lower body was preserved, exposing the insides of the lower pelvic cavity.

His legs and boots looked normal as they laid flat upon the ground protruding away from the fire.

"What are we going to do with that?" Everett cried.

"Shut your mouth, Everett," Adel said firmly. "The boss will tell us what he wants."

Singleton, already awake, listened to the men's bickering. He walked up the incline toward their camp.

"Boys, bury that," he said as if he were talking about planting a garden. "Come up here when you're finished," he said.

Pegram and Bohanan buried the remains of Otis Cullum. They said a short prayer, and then hurried back to camp.

Singleton was brewing a pot of coffee over the fire further up the ridge. He poured three cups as they approached with small shovels in hand.

"Takes strong men to complete worthy tasks," Singleton said as he handed the bitter, black coffee to his last two men. "Yes?" he looked into their eyes.

"Yes sir," both men chided in response, almost trying to beat one another to the appropriate answer.

"You two *girls* won't let me down," he said insulting them as he picked up his own cup, never looking their direction.

The temperature of the metal coffee cup blistered Jack's bottom lip, but he didn't flinch. The boiling coffee scalded every portion of his mouth as he drank, which only cemented his hate for Revel Knox.

Leadership required a unique set of skills; skills that conveyed physical toughness, along with abilities that seemed to go beyond mortal men. Abilities like killing without empathy, gutting men as if they were animals. Abilities that never allowed other men to see fear, weakness, or kindness toward the cowardly.

Jack *was* that man. He was a hardened man who knew that leadership required steely determination in every situation.

"Sir, we won't let you down," his men admitted.

Jack was pleased to hear those words. He would find Revel Knox… if it was the last thing he would ever do.

Chapter 8

Arthur Meade sat at the center of his customary VIP table eating a late dinner with local law colleagues at the Housebridge Theatre Company, just a few blocks down the street from his office. Housebridge was a combination restaurant, saloon, and theatre.

Meade laughed at his colleague's jokes while sipping a glass of white wine. He smoked their cigars and patronized their pretentiousness. Arthur Meade looked, one the outside, like a successful and prominent lawyer going places. He had a beautiful wife, a fine three story Victorian home just off of the town's square, a successful law practice, and all of the material trappings that accommodated his type of lifestyle and success.

But on the inside, Arthur hated every minute of his miserable life. He hated the practice of law. He hated the mundane routine that was required of him. He hated the files, the tedious hours of note-taking, and the young men who pretended to be his friends, while simultaneously trying to take his clients and reputation.

Arthur hated his civil responsibilities to the community: endless ribbon-cutting ceremonies, political Galas, fundraisers, and the like.

And he hated his wife, Abigail; stupid, naïve, Abigail. Their marriage had been pre-arranged by their respective families. Abigail sought nothing more than to be a celebrity socialite and she loved the *idea* of being married to a successful attorney... but behind closed doors she was little more than a roommate to Arthur.

Arthur Ignatius Meade believed that he was above these small-minded mid-westerners. He believed himself to be a blue-blood, above the law, and all of those involved in the system of law. Somewhere along the line he had been cheated in life, or so he thought. *Just another cog in the machine*, he thought to himself. *I was meant for greatness – not small town politics. But that is about to change...*

Arthur smiled to himself as he puffed on the fine cigar. His thoughts were on incredible riches and freedom… he could hardly contain his excitement!

He felt chills of excitement at the thought of leaving all of this behind – leaving his wife, his home, his practice, and this small town life.

He envisioned traveling in warm tropical climates with young beautiful women, absent of his nagging wife and the responsibilities of life. He would live as a prince, and indulge his every desire. It was a life he knew he deserved. Only one obstacle stood between him and his dreams. It was an obstacle by the name of Revel Knox.

The theatre was into their third act, the restaurant was packed, and the volume of the restaurant chatter competed against the performance on the stage. The saloon was also full of patrons; loud, noisy, obnoxious folks who cared not for theatre or fine food.

"Gentleman," Arthur stood from his seat. "I trust that you will all forgive me, but I must defray myself from our truly enjoyable meal as another poor soul needs my attention."

"Here, here, good man! Be gone with you then!" One of his drunken colleagues raised a glass to Arthur and the group laughed in unison.

"Oh," said the well-dressed man to Arthur's left, "I believe I see the poor soul who needs your attention." The group looked toward the woman who had captured Arthur's gaze. It was Isabel, the theatre company's lead actress.

"Now, now, gentleman," Arthur said as he buttoned his suit-coat, "I would have you only to meditate upon the kindest thoughts of our professional relationship. She simply needs the *best* lawyer, which is why I am the *only* one at this table that she has retained."

Everyone at Arthur's table laughed loudly, some raising their glasses to him as he stepped away from his chair. *Laugh now, my friends*, Arthur thought as he walked away.

"Isabel," Arthur said to her as he paused at her half-opened dressing room door. She turned quickly, recognized him and ran to him.

"Ignatius! My heart leaps for joy in seeing your face!" She kissed his cheeks, forehead, and lips. Isabel was half his age. Arthur had financially supported her for almost a year… what an expensive year it had been.

Arthur had showered her with lavish gifts and cash. He paid her monthly rent on her small town-home and spared no expense in meeting her every whim.

"Darling, meet me at the Jefferson City Drake Hotel this evening at 1:00am. We will spend the night together in frolic and fun!"

"Oh, Ignatius, you are all that I have thought about!" she said between kisses. Her Spanish accent increased his lust. "I will see you there!"

Chapter 9

Revel leaned against a tanning post eating a piece of freshly baked bread. Millie read a story in the Shawnokwan language to several children around the large campfire. He looked up and admired the stars in the night sky.

Revel's body was sore, but he marveled at how quickly he had healed. The Indian women had worked oils into his body several times each day, and it had been very unpleasant; however, it was the first time in his life that he had not developed an infection from gunshot wounds, and the first time he had healed *this* quickly.

He was also surprised at his ability to walk without a limp. Revel had spent that morning deer-hunting with a group of Shawnokwan men. He figured that they had walked over 6 miles. The hunt resulted in the harvest of a small spike-buck and three does.

"*Maybe I died at that waterfall,*" he mused to himself, "*and maybe **this** is Heaven – Heaven is full of*

Indians! Maybe that's why this bread is so good!" He smiled at the thoughts.

These people were fascinating, but also confusing. The Shawnokwan were a living contrast to everything that he had ever heard about Native Americans. His violent experiences as a young man with the Shawnee had formed his previous negative perception about Native Americans, but the Shawnokwan people had caused him to rethink his entire thought process about their race and culture.

"You look much better," Millie said with a smile as she walked toward him.

"I bet you say that to all your patients," Revel replied with a sheepish grin.

Millie laughed. "No, only to the patients that act like big babies!" She laughed harder.

"Hey, it wasn't an act!" Revel said as seriously as he could. "I come from a long line of big babies!"

Her laughs caught the attention some of the women walking by, so she regained her composure.

"So, Mr. Knox–"

"Yes, Ms. Echoa," he quickly responded. Millie was caught off guard by his remembrance and perfect pronunciation of her Indian name… and impressed, needless to say.

"Uh, I forgot what I was going to say," Millie admitted, causing them to laugh in unison.

"Some big babies are smarter than other big babies," Revel said with a grin.

They looked at each other. The mutual attraction was undeniable.

"Oh, I was going to say," Millie looked away from his eyes, "you're welcome to stay as long as you like."

Revel looked down at the ground and pushed on a pebble with his boot.

"I would love to stay, but every day I am here brings more danger to you – *all* of you."

Millie couldn't hide her disappointment, but her concern for the Shawnokwan far outweighed her new feelings for this man.

"I appreciate your unselfish concern, Mr. Knox," she replied. "When are you leaving?"

"I need to buy a horse and a saddle from your elders–"

"They will *give* you everything you need, but they won't accept your money," Millie interupted.

"They won't accept my money–"

"No, no," she interrupted again as she stepped closer. "Mr. Knox, our faith teaches us to provide for those in need. You have need of a horse and supplies, so we will provide for your needs," she said as she put her hand on his hand.

"Millie, I don't take charity–"

"Mr. Knox, you are obliged to take God's blessings with thankfulness," she interrupted a third time.

"So why would God be helping me now?" Revel asked as he looked into her eyes.

"Maybe He's trying to get your attention, Mr. Knox," she responded. "Good night." She squeezed his hand, turned quickly and walked away from Revel's tent.

Revel laid comfortably in the darkness of the teepee. The furs that composed his mattress were soft and warm. The knitted blankets covering his body smelled like Eucalyptus. He had put two logs on the fire before getting into bed. The August nights tended to get cool in this region.

His body needed sleep, but his mind reeled. Singleton wouldn't give up. He had to get back to Jefferson City. The Shawnokwans were in danger because of his presence. And Arthur Meade… the thought of Meade made his blood boil. A reckoning was coming…

Chapter 10

"Where's Singleton," Everett asked Bohanan. Singleton's last two men stood around the camp-fire in the evening's darkness.

"Don't know," Bohanan said without emotion as he lit a cigarette. "He went off at dusk with his long-rifle. Who knows what he's thinking," he said as he spit into the fire.

Everett took a sip from his flask. "Been at this spot three weeks now. What are we doin' here?"

"Well," Bohanan said as he took a drag, "We both know that Jack is convinced Revel Knox is hurt, but still alive – "

"Adel, Revel Knox's body could be washed down to New Mexico by now!" Everett Pegram exclaimed with frustration.

"Then what course of action do *you* suggest we pursue, Mr. Pegram," Adel replied as he slowly scanned the darkness of the forest line.

"Ah–!" Everett Pegram cursed as he threw his empty flask into the woods and stomped down to the river's edge.

Bohanan flipped his cigarette into the fire. He wasn't concerned about Everett Pegram's temper-tantrums. What concerned him was Jack Singleton.

What happened to the last man who filled his belly with liquor and cursed Jack Singleton? Adel thought to himself as he looked down the hill at Pegram who had stopped at the river's edge.

Everett Pegram's desperation was growing. He tossed a stick into the fast flowing river.

"I ain't dying out here for this," Pegram said softly to himself. His horse was ready for the ride, tied to a tree far behind their tent. Pegram had previously stowed away some of the remaining venison and beans inside his saddlebags. With Bohanan up at the fire and Singleton gone, it was time to go.

He slipped down the river and circled back to his horse through the trees. His horse snorted at his approach.

"Shhh, shhh, easy girl," he coaxed his horse as he approached. "We'll be out of here in no time," he said softly to her..

Pegram untied the leather leads from the small sapling and quietly mounted his horse. She jerked a little at first, then relaxed. The leather saddle snapped and popped as he took control of the horse. He pulled the reigns slightly to the right, turning her out of the brush and into an open path.

He rubbed his spurs gently against her skin, feeling the distance between the stirrups and her body. Everett was free! Free from the madman, Singleton. Free from the fear he felt in Singleton's presence, and free from this ridiculous goose-chase!

Everett grasped the reigns tightly and pushed both boots forward, ready to kick the spurs back into the sides of his Mustang, but the Mustang unexpectedly reared up in a violent stand, falling completely backward onto Everett's body. The horse rolled off of him to the right, and Everett gasped for air.

His entire chest felt crushed and his pelvis was surely broken. He couldn't feel his legs.

Everett, lying on his back, rolled his head to the right so that he could see his horse. She gimp-jumped, but couldn't get to her feet. Blood poured from her rear-right hip. How could that be? It looked like a long cut down her–

The flash of metal in the moonlight pierced the horse's skull. Her body jerked violently for a brief moment and then she laid still… dead. Everett's emotions and hatred grew instantly hot. Killing a horse went against every fiber of Everett's being.

"Mr. Pegram," said Jack Singleton. Everett closed his eyes and listened to Jack's boot-steps draw closer. "I apologize for the need to incapacitate your mode of transportation, but your actions were giving me the distinct feeling that you might be leaving our party."

Everett took shallow breaths, struggling with his body's inability to breathe. The pain in his pelvic area was insufferable. Tears formed in the corners of his eyes.

"Mr. Singleton, I just need to get back to my family," Everett said in desperation.

"Now, Mr. Pegram, is it your belief that I am the kind of man who would prevent your patriarchal duties to family?" Singleton said as he squatted down at Everett's left shoulder.

"No,sir, no, sir…" Everett's words trailed off.

"Everett," Jack said as he pulled the injured man upward toward a sitting position. Everett screamed out in pain. "Let's get you back to camp where we can mend your wounds."

Everett's saw a flicker of hope that his life would be spared.

"Do you really think that I can capture Revel Knox without you?" Jack asked Everett as he helped him sit up.

"Well, sir, you need me –"

Pain interrupted Everett's reply as shock his body. Jack had plunged his knife into Everett's right kidney. Everett couldn't breathe. He couldn't make a sound.

Singleton, using his right hand, sunk the knife into Everett all the way to the hilt of the blade. Everett gasped for air and squirmed to get away, but his strength evaporated.

"Mr. Pegram," Jack said through clinched teeth into Pegram's left ear as he held Pegram around the neck with his left arm. "Your betrayal and cowardice is now rewarded." Jack twisted the knife a quarter turn. Everett's body jolted outward, causing Jack to squeeze down on Everett's neck.

Pegram's body grew limp as Jack breathed heavy into Pegram's ear. Jack could smell the expelled urine and bile from Pegram's body as he died.

Jack stood to survey the dead horse and his dead employee. He cared nothing for Pegram or his horse. Coyotes and varmints would clean up the mess.

Chapter 11

Jack Singleton appeared at the campfire scaring Adel Bohanan half to death. Adel was his last remaining crew member.

"Boss, where you been?" Bohanan asked with trepidation.

"Knox is alive. He is staying at the Shawnokwan's encampment," Singleton said as he poured a cup of stale coffee from the pot that had been over the fire far too long.

Bohanan listened to his boss with a sense of awe and fear.

"Tomorrow we will watch his movements from the eastern ridgeline to see if he leaves that Indian camp by himself. When he does, we'll kill him," Singleton stated flatly while taking a drink from his cup.

"Where's Pegram?" Adel asked timidly.

"Pegram has gone to the abode of cowards. Would you like to join him, Mr. Bohanan?" Singleton's steely eyes focused on Bohanan.

Adel searched for courage and ignored Jack's direct question.

"So, it's just you and me?" Adel asked Jack.

"Looks like," Singleton replied.

"Two is enough," Adel offered. "Three's a crowd. Besides, I never liked him anyway." Bohanan replied as he stared into Singleton's eyes. Adel had found his courage.

"And Mr. Singleton," Adel pulled the shirt from his body as he spoke to Jack. "If you're going to kill me, let's get it over with right now," Adel Bohanan said as he unlatched his gun belt. It dropped to the ground. Adel then pulled out his knife and held it toward Jack's direction, assuming a knife-fighter's stance.

An evil smile spread across Jack's face. His eyes twinkled as he unbuckled his heavy gun belt, throwing it toward the tent. Jack yanked his knife from its sheathe and felt a surge of nervous energy fill his veins.

Adel swayed back and forth trying to anticipate Singleton's attack.

"My young friend," said Jack in an ominous tone. "Engaging a man of courage is a glorious thing–"

"You gonna work that steak knife," Adel interrupted, "or talk me to death–"

Adel's question was interrupted by the speed of Jack's arm. He heard the spin of Jack's knife as it passed his ear, penetrating the trunk of a wild cedar a few yards behind him.

"*Unarmed!*" Adel exclaimed in his mind, but Jack Singleton had already lunged toward Adel and was now in mid-air over the campfire.

Adel swung the knife in his right hand toward Jack's temple, but he was a tenth of a second late. His knife passed over Jack's head as Jack landed and dropped down in front of him.

Adel's body turned slightly from the momentum of his wild swing. Jack saw Adel's imbalance and, in a split second, kicked Adel's foot out from under him. Adel toppled to the ground.

Jack jumped on top of Adel the moment he hit the ground. They groaned, kicked, and wrestled for control of the knife in Adel's hand.

Adel punched Jack in the head with his left fist as Jack grappled to get the knife out of Adel's right hand. Adel punched Jack's head repeatedly, but Jack didn't seem to be affected by the blows.

The two men wrestled on the ground; both now covered with one another's sweat, spit, and blood. Adel saw the blood.

Thoughts raced through Adel's mind. *"Jack is bleeding. Losing my grip. He's going to get the knife–"*

Adel saw a quick flicker of fire-light refecting from something... Jack's knife stuck in the Cedar. His grip on his own knife was almost gone, and he knew his life would go with his grip.

Adel inhaled a deep breath, yelled out as loudly as he could and bucked Jack off of his body. Jack was thrown to the side, but he now had Adel's knife.

Jack tiredly picked himself up from the ground and looked toward Adel's position. Adel had retrieved the knife from the tree trunk and was coming quickly toward Jack.

"*Tired of playing,*" Jack thought to himself. Adel screamed as he lunged at Jack's stomach with the long knife. Adel had him, but Jack blocked Adel, causing sparks to fly from the clash of blades.

Jack followed with a rapid body-spin, enabling him to get behind Adel. He brought the blade Adel's throat.

"Do it!" screamed Adel. "What are you waiting for? Just kill me!"

Jack began to laugh. He removed the knife from Adel's throat and shoved the young man to the ground.

"Mr. Bohanan," Jack said through laughter and exasperation. "I am deeply impressed by your courage and skill."

Adel got up from the ground and looked at Jack. Both men were filthy and covered with blood.

"Boy," Jack continued, "You had better wash that ear to prevent infection."

Adel felt of his left ear. The blood covering both men was *Adel's* blood. Jack's knife-throw had sliced the center of the cartilage of Adel's ear.

Adel began to laugh with Jack. Both men were exhausted and relieved to be alive.

"Yes, sir," Adel replied as he walked toward the river.

"And, Mr. Bohanan," Jack got Adel's attention.

"What, boss?" Adel asked as he turned back toward Jack.

"That's *my* knife in your hand, boy!"

Jack Singleton threw a few pieces of deadwood into the fire, then used a rag to clean his face and neck. He had gained a genuine respect for Adel Bohanan.

Adel was snoring on his bedroll while Jack leaned against a boulder far away from the campfire considering his plan...

"One man left. Bohanan will help me kill Knox, and then I'll kill Bohanan. Meade's financial reward will be mine alone."

Chapter 12

Isabel awoke early and bathed. She proceeded to make coffee while Arthur slept soundly in her bed. The morning sunlight shone through the windows of their second-floor room.

She poured two cups of coffee, added honey to both, then a little cream to hers.

"Sweetheart," she said in her Spanish accent. "Time to wake up!"

Arthur Meade opened his eyes to the sound of her delicate voice. "What time is it?" he asked lazily.

"Quarter past six," Isabel responded after retrieving his pocket-watch from the side table.

"Thank you," Arthur replied as he sat up in bed.

"Can we play today, Mr. Meade," she asked as if she were a little girl asking her daddy to take her to the park.

"No, Isabel, we cannot," Arthur said as he raised from the bed and scratched his head. "I simply have too much to do today."

"You are no fun!" she said, pouting from the end of the bed. "Should you like me to stay in this room all day waiting for you?" Isabel was emotional.

"No. Go enjoy your day."

"Without you?" She looked at him with her bottom lip poked out.

"Without me," he said apologetically. "But I plan to see you tonight," said Arthur with a smile.

"Where are you taking me?" Isabel asked with renewed excitement.

"I'm going to take you to place where the food is unique and the music is excellent!" He said.

"I knew you loved me!" Isabel blurted as she jumped toward Arthur from the end of the bed.

"What shall I wear?" She questioned while kissing his cheeks.

"The black evening dress," he offered.

"Yes, what a good idea!" she responded as she ran to her clothing trunk. "You will be delighted with me, no?" She looked at Arthur.

"Delight is not a strong enough word for you, princess!" Arthur said with a smile.

Arthur cleaned up, shaved, and put on the same suit he'd worn the night before. Who cared? He enjoyed his sin with Isabel. It was a life that he craved.

That evening they ate smoked bass with almond potatoes and sipped eleven-year-old Brandy. A concerto of violinists played in the background. Isabel, who had consumed far more Brandy than food, was drunk.

"Isabel, our plan is almost ready," Arthur said after taking a sip.

"We will go away together, yes?" Her eyes brightened as her smile grew.

"Yes, we will," Arthur smiled in return. He leaned forward and lowered his voice, "And we will have so much money that the entire world will be at our beck-and-call."

"How much will we have, darling?" Isabel was always excited when the conversation turned toward the promise of Arthur's money.

"More than you can count, Isabel," Arthur replied with a grin.

But his grin disappeared as his thoughts turned towrd Jack Singleton and Revel Knox.

Revel Knox had to be killed… and so did Jack Singleton.

Chapter 13

Revel washed his face from water in a clay pot inside his tent. *"That is the strangest smelling soap,"* he thought to himself as he scrubbed his long beard in a circular motion.

Millie had just visited Revel's tent, bringing coffee and cornbread. He hugged and thanked her at his open tent-flap. Their affection for one another was growing.

"Mr. Knox?" And Indian with a thick Shawnokwan accent said from outside the teepee a few moments later.

Revel stepped through the flap in the early morning's light. He was now thirty years old, with a lean, strong 6' 2" frame, broader than average shoulders, light brown hair and intense eyes. His physical appearance and the confidence he possessed intimidated most men.

"Yes?" he replied.

"There are two white men watching our camp from the upper chateau. We believe," the Indian continued, "that these are the men you spoke of," said the middle-aged Shawnokwan man who spoke to Revel in perfect English. The Shawnokwans taught their children both languages from birth.

"Only two? Are you sure?" Revel wiped his face as he fought the temptation to look toward the ridgeline.

"Yes, only two. The others are dead," the Indian replied. "Our scouts have reported killings among their group."

"Killings?" Revel's eyes narrowed.

"Their leader is killing them," the Indian man said with equal confusion.

"Can your men describe their leader?" Revel asked. The Indian man gave a detailed description.

"Yeah, that's Jack Singleton alright," Revel said as he pulled the twist tobacco from his pocket.

"Thank you, Quello," Knox said as he turned toward his tent.

"Mr. Knox," Quello stopped Revel. "What would you have us do about the men watching us?"

"Nothing. Their *fear* of you will keep them at a good distance, for now."

Quello considered Revel's words. "Prayer first, Mr. Knox," he said sincerely. "Let us speak again when the sun is mid-sky. Agree?"

Revel nodded his head, not expecting Quello's suggestion of prayer. Quello walked away as Revel stepped back into the teepee. Revel had a fleeting thought that he could actually *feel* Jack Singleton's eyes on him.

Chapter 14

Singleton and Bohanan lay in a prose position among tall weeds at the edge of the high chateau, watching the camp through refractive telescopes supplied by Meade.

"Chiggers are eating me alive," Bohanan cursed and scratched at his rear-end. Singleton peered through the scope watching Knox talk to the Indian below. He imagined the satisfaction of gutting Revel like a hog.

"Knox is communing with *Indians*," Singleton said in a low, disgusted tone as he continued to peer through the scope.

"I never seen anything like it," Bohanan was as bewildered as Singleton. "I could get him with my long–"

Bohanan's suggestion was interrupted by a punch to the side of his head.

"Are you that stupid?" Singleton looked sideways at Bohanan as Bohanan rubbed his face.

"You want several hundred Indians on top of you in seconds, just squeeze off a round from that long rifle."

Singleton looked back through the scope. "That Indian is leaving. Knox is going back into the teepee," Singleton narrated what he saw. Adel didn't want another punch upside the head, so he didn't say a word.

Jack pushed the scope together and slipped it into his hip pocket, slowly rising to a squatting position. Adel followed his lead.

"We have got to draw him out," said Jack as he watched the valley below. "And I believe we have seen the bait that will lure him."

"What is the bait?" asked Adel.

Jack turned to Adel causing Adel to pull his head back in anticipation of another blow.

"What lures *every* man, Mr. Bohanan?" Jack asked with a grin.

Bohanan smiled.

Chapter 15

The Jefferson City Annual Town Hall Meeting was about to begin. Arthur Meade was in his element, glad-handing local politicians and the people of influence.

"Hello, Mr. Meade! Wonderful to see you again, old friend," Said Harry Benefot as he shook Arthur's hand with excitement.

"Equally pleased, Mr. Benefot," Arthur smiled.

"I believe at least a thousand grace us this evening," Benefot suggested with smiles and waves to the enormous crowd gathering around the city's Rhineland Park Gazebo.

"Eleven hundred thus far, Mr. Benefot," Arthur replied. "We have counters."

"Ah, Arthur, you are always one step ahead," laughed Harry, "

Arthur smiled and bowed his head slightly in appreciation. "*You have no idea*," thought Meade as Harry Benefot went to take his seat.

Fourteen of the most prominent men of Jefferson City sat in finely crafted wooden chairs positioned in a semi-circle fashion under the gazebo roof facing the large audience, directly behind a center podium that faced the crowd.

Arthur sat in his assigned chair just to the left rear of the podium. The mayor of Jefferson City was at the podium giving his State of the County address.

Arthur looked past the mayor's backside out into the audience. He scanned the hundreds of faces in the crowd, and smiled by his recognition of the dozens upon dozens of German Immigrants that had, and continued to, make him rich.

He also saw many German widows in the audience: women whose husbands had been murdered at his command. Meade had accumulated sixteen vineyards totaling four hundred and eleven acres of land, creating a huge source of annual income for himself.

He saw the relatives of entire German families who had burned to death in house fires – fires orchestrated by Meade. Seven families had perished in Meade's fires, which had netted him close to $160,000.00.

Meade shifted his legs, trying to find another comfortable position in his chair, completely bored by the drone of the mayor's voice. He pulled out his pocket watch. 6:22pm.

Charles Oliver patted Arthur on the knee and looked at Arthur with a smug grin as the mayor mentioned Arthur in his speech. Arthur whispered a "thank you" to Mr. Oliver who sat in the chair immediately to his right.

Charles Oliver was the President of Old Dominion Bank – Jefferson City's one and only banking institution, and Arthur Meade was on the bank board. Arthur's position with the board gave him access and influence to the inner workings of Jefferson City's financial infrastructure. This access and influence was the engine of Meade's schemes.

"*When will this asinine speech expire*," Arthur thought to himself. "*I need a drink*."

His thoughts shifted from boredom to anxiety.

"*Find Knox and find that notebook. Destroy* them both."

Chapter 16

Revel and Millie sat together at the fire. The ground was still wet from the day's rain and the night sky was overcast.

She had studied the Bible with him for several days. Revel had not been a "religious" man, but he believed in God. He also regretted many of his past decisions.

Furthermore, there had been a void in his heart. He had never been able to put a finger on it, but something was *missing* from his life. He had tried filling the void with gold, women, booze, cards, cattle drives – anything that would occupy an ambitious, and sometimes idle, mind.

Nothing had worked. As a matter of fact, most of the things he had hoped would fill the void in his heart had back-fired.

Revel Knox was not a *bad* man. His parents had instilled a good moral compass into his heart at an early age. He was simply an *empty* man, as most men of his generation were. Revel's world was filled with the business of life, but the busy worldly life had never given him any real satisfaction.

He was, in addition, an accomplished man: a degree in business from Boston College, a successful cattleman, and the beneficiary of 3000 acres of the finest land found in all of Missouri: Jefferson City's Rhineland grounds.

Still yet, his soul hungered for something more... something that would fill the hole in his heart.

Revel was now finding *that* something.

"How is this possible?" Revel asked her, marveling over the thought.

"It's the providence of God," she replied.

"But *Indians* being *Christians*?" He was perplexed. Most Indians believed in polytheism (many gods).

"I know," she replied. "Mr. Knox – "

"Please call me Revel," he interrupted while putting his hand on hers.

"Okay… Revel," she smiled back at him. "My grandfather, Orvel, settled in this area long ago and developed a close relationship with the Shawnokwan tribe. He married a Shawnokwan woman, and then spent many years learning the Shawnokwan language.

"In turn, Orvel taught them the English language using the New Testament as the tool for teaching.

"Conversely, the elders of the tribe commissioned grandfather to translate the New Testament into the Shawnokwan language. It took Orvel approximately two years to transcribe the entire New Testament into the Shawnokwan tongue."

Revel listened with sincere amazement.

"Revel, grandfather taught us the gospel and how we are to respond to Christ's gospel in the same way first century Christians responded[*]. That *one* man is responsible for thousands of our people becoming Christians," Millie said.

"That is remarkable," Revel said aloud as he looked at the campfire.

"But that's not important, Revel," Millie pulled at Revel's hand. He looked back at her.

"What is important is *your* understanding of the gospel of Jesus Christ," she looked intently into his eyes.

"Do you believe that Jesus Christ is the son of God?"

Revel considered her question.

"Yes, Millie, I believe that. I've always believed that," Revel said.

"Do you believe that God raised Him from the dead?" She asked the second question.

"Yeah, I believe that He did," Revel said with conviction.

Millie couldn't control herself. She threw her arms around him as they sat on the hand-hewn bench positioned close to the fire. "Thank you, Father," she whispered a prayer of thanks into Revel's ear.

Tears formed in Revel's eyes. Embarrassment overcame his mind – he wasn't a man accustomed to *crying*.

"Revel, every bad thing you have ever done and every sin you have ever committed can be forgiven by God through Christ's sacrifice on the cross. God's love and grace for you is found in Jesus Christ's willingness to die for you and the blood He voluntarily shed on the cross! All you have to do is to *trust* in Christ's blood."

"I need to be baptized for the forgiveness of my sins," Revel admitted. "All of the passages you've shown me tonight... Millie, I'm ready."

A large group of Shawnokwan men and women were gathered at the edge of the river. An elder of the tribe stood with Revel in waist-deep water. The night sky was overcast, with no moonlight, making it difficult to see the two men in the river.

"Revel Knox," the Shawnokwan elder said in a volume that all who gathered could hear. "Do you believe that Jesus Christ is the Son of God?"

"I do," Revel said through tears.

"I now baptize you for the forgiveness of your sins, according to the Bible, in the name of the Father, the Son, and the Holy Spirit[*]."

The elder baptized Revel and the Shawnokwans who were gathered at the river's edge cheered in their native language. God added another soul to the church of Christ[*]. He was received with hugs and kisses from his new brethren in Christ.

"Oh, Revel," Millie clutched him tightly. "You are now my brother in the Lord."

He squeezed her in return and fought back tears. "I owe you my eternal life, Millie," he whispered into her ear.

"No, no. Your debt is to Jesus Christ, not me," she whispered back. She wept with joy as the emotion of the event overwhelmed her heart.

"Millie," Revel whispered as they held their embrace.

"Yes," she replied.

"You are now my sister?" he asked into her ear.

"Yes," she squeezed him tighter.

"I have never had these kinds of feelings for a *sister*," he said into her ear with a grin.

She couldn't control her outburst of laughter at what he had said. The group sang hymns as they walked back to the camp.

Jack Singleton sheathed his knife and crept quietly back to his horse. He had watched the event in the darkness, some fifty feet away on the opposite side of the river. Jack had strongly considered entering the river and killing both men with his blade, but decided that the plan wouldn't give him the personal satisfaction he sought.

"Religion won't save you, Mr. Knox," he said under his breath as he worked his way back to camp through the darkness. "I'll have your head on a stick before this is finished."

* Acts 2:36-47; Acts 20:28; Romans 16:16; Colossians 1:18

Chapter 17

Jack Singleton, now back at camp, stood at the edge of the campfire watching the last survivor of his crew sleep. He added a few broken pieces of deadwood to the embers and rolled a cigarette.

Singleton took a second drag from his freshly rolled smoke and thought of his dead brother, Bristol. Bristol had been the only family he had left, and Bristol's death would be avenged.

A third puff… Adel snored in the background. Jack thought of the $10,000.00 Meade would give him upon his arrival in Jefferson City with Knox's dead body. He began to spend the money in his mind. He relished the thought of twisting his knife in Revel's dying body, and rehearsed the words that he would say to him during the remaining moments of Revel's life.

Jack had not always been the man he was now. He had spent a career enforcing the law of the land, trying his best to defend the innocent and fighting those who sought after evil.

He flipped what remained of his cigarette into the fire and sat down next to its edge. His body ached from age and hard living.

Jack's former strong physique and handsome face had faded over time. His skin was weatherworn and his body had atrophied mildly. Jack was now, at 5' 11", 175 lbs., and forty-nine years old, feeling much older than his years.

Jack's dark, handlebar-mustache was a contrast to his salt and pepper hair. His body had grown leaner with age. His current overall appearance was that of an old lawman, but with a youthful, steely-eyed determination.

His long black overcoat covered a white, button-down shirt that was overlain by a gray wool four button vest. He wore dark gray riding pants tucked into black leather boots, but Jack never wore a hat of any kind. Hats, in his opinion, hindered focus. They shielded the sun, but were encumbrances in almost every activity.

"*Knox can't stay with the Indians forever,*" he thought to himself as he sat by the fire. Bohanan continued to snore.

"*Capture the woman? Draw him into the forest and kill him?*" Jack played potential scenarios in his mind.

"*No. Wait until he packs his horse for the next leg of the trip. Get him far away from the Indians and kill him in the wilderness? Yes, that'll work.*"

His gaze shifted to Bohanan who slept soundly a few feet away.

Singleton stood up, walked over to Bohanan sleeping next to the campfire, lifted his Colt out of the holster, pulled back the hammer and fired a single round into Bohanan's head.

The shot echoed loudly against the hillside surrounding the camp.

"*Mr. Bohanan,*" Jack thought to himself as he watched blood trickle from the bullet hole. "*My respect for you has prevented your suffering.*"

His weekly salary instantly increased for a for a fourth time. He would continue to bill Arthur Meade weekly for all four men's salaries, plus his own, and pocket it all. Jack's objective was to take Knox alone – a plan he had devised several weeks prior.

Jack rolled another cigarette as he squatted next to Bohanan's dead body. He licked the paper and pressed it to the roll.

"You deserve to be buried properly," Jack said to Adel's dead body. He shoved a stick into the hot embers, then pulled it out revealing a small flame flaring at the tip and lit his home-rolled smoke.

"Mr. Knox, it is now just you and I," Jack said aloud as he tossed the stick back into the fire.

He retrieved his pack-shovel and began to dig.

Revel was startled from sleep by the sound of the gun-shot rolling across the hills. He reached for his Cooper. Tension filled his body as he lay quietly in the darkness of the teepee…

Chapter 18

Meade sat at his desk reviewing Jack Singleton's latest telegram. It had arrived at 7:08am from from the Fort Collins Western Union office. The telegram said:

Found Knox alive, stop. Knox collaborating with Shawnokwan Tribe, stop. Knox hiding in Shawnokwan camp, stop.

Must wait on Knox to leave camp, stop. Will kill Knox subsequent to his departure from Shawnokwan camp, stop.

Wire check for arrears salaries owed to self and team to this location, a.s.a.p., stop.

Jack Singleton

Arthur rubbed at his beard as he studied Jack's telegram. He was not troubled by the information revealed in the telegram. He was troubled by what had *not* been revealed.

Jack' correspondences had increased in vagueness of detail over the past four weeks – a fact that had not escaped Arthur.

He then picked up a second telegram from his desk, also originating from Fort Collins. It was a message that had arrived just prior to Jack's telegram. The time stamp said 6:41am that morning. It said:

```
Tracked & located Jack
Singleton per your request,
stop.

Singleton is alone, stop.
Repeat:
Singleton is alone, stop.

Found remains of three in
party and gravesite of
fourth, stop. Please advise,
stop.
```

S. Underwood

Samuel Underwood was Arthur Meade's "back-up" plan. Arthur had not achieved his wealth and prominence by being stupid. He was a man that inspected what he expected; therefore, Samuel Underwood was an instrument of insurance against Jack Singleton.

Underwood was an expert tracker and mountain man, and he could find almost anyone or anything for the right price. When Jack Singleton's messages became obtuse, Arthur wasted no time in finding a man who would track Singleton and report his movements.

Meade's investment into Underwood was now paying off. Jack was hiding something, as Arthur suspected, and had gone rogue.

"Ms. Townsend," Arthur called to his secretary. She stepped into his office and he handed her an envelope.

"Take this to the Western Union and have the contents telegraphed to Fort Collins immediately," Arthur commanded as he stood and collected his coat and briefcase. "And cancel all of my afternoon appointments." Arthur's no-nonsense tone put a little steam into her step.

Chapter 19

Revel lit a candle in his teepee and checked the pocket watch given to him by the Shawnokwan Chief. It was an item highly valued by the Chief, previously obtained through trading Aquamarine crystals native to the Colorado Mountains. It was 4:05am.

The joy and peace he felt in his heart surpassed anything he had ever experienced. The hole in his heart was filled with God's promises. But Revel was also torn by anxiety that Jack was so close to the camp. The Shawnokwans were in danger and he knew that a quick departure was now inevitable.

Revel opened the Bible that Millie had given him and researched his notes from their previous Bible studies.

Revel, on his knees, prayed fervently that God would give him the strength he needed to do what he now knew had to be done.

The passages of Christ's words (verses that teach every follower of Christ how to treat enemies and how to react to violence) were the most difficult for Revel.

"Singleton is waiting for his opportunity. I've got to get back to Jefferson City. I can cover about 20 miles a day through the hills and scrubs. At twenty miles a day, it'll take about six weeks," Revel thought to himself. He felt for the key in that hidden pants-pocket one last time.

At 4:35am he mounted the Appaloosa given to him by the elders of the tribe. The leather saddle felt broken-in and surprisingly comfortable. His saddlebags, packed by several of his Shawnokwan sisters in Christ, were filled with dried venison, salt, berries, and nuts. They had included a bow and drill for fire-starting, flutes filled with essential oils for injuries, and two skinning knives made by one of the men.

His Cooper revolver was now in his right holster. His grandfather's knife felt good strapped to his thigh. A long rifle rested in a scabbard at the front side of the saddle.

Millie handed him another revolver. "I pray you don't have to use this, Revel, but for safety's sake please take it," she whispered to him. It was an 1862 Colt, .36 caliber police model with a four-and-a-half-inch barrel. It was a gun-fighter's pistol and a gift that he would never forget.

"This is my kind of pistol." He smiled at the thought.

"Millie… I can't seem to find the words–"

"Revel," she softly interrupted "You do not need to say a thing." She reached up as high as she could to hug him as he leaned down from the saddle.

He embraced her with one arm while trying to still his horse with the other. Revel inhaled the smell of her hair and whispered his gratefulness into her ear.

"Millie, you saved my life and you saved my soul–"

"Revel, Jesus Christ and your obedience to His word has saved your soul, *not* me," she whispered.

The Appaloosa snorted and stomped her front hoof.

"Jealous horse," whispered Revel with a grin. Millie laughed and wiped the tears from her cheeks as Revel raised back up in the saddle.

"God go with you, Revel Knox," she stepped away from his horse while staring into his eyes.

"You, too," he said as he gently bounced his boot heels off of the horse's side. Revel rode out of camp toward Jefferson City – a journey that would span approximately 800 miles.

Jack Singleton stood on the ground in a Pine grove about a hundred and twenty paces to the west of Revel's position. He held the reigns of his horse, stroking his horse's muzzle as he watched.

"Shhh," Jack said gently to his horse, keeping the horse quiet and calm. After Revel rode a short distance away from Millie, Jack climbed gingerly into his saddle and followed. He felt that rush of the capture…

Samuel Underwood, just a hundred and fifty yards behind Jack Singleton, felt that *same* rush!

Chapter <u>20</u>

Revel bathed after sunset in the cool waters of the Arkansas River about 100 miles northeast of Dodge City, Kansas.

He was now at the half-way point back to Jefferson City, Missouri and it had taken him longer than he originally planned.

"*Twenty-six days*," he thought to himself. Knox had, at this point, successfully skirted two bears, a band of rough-neck outlaws, one cougar and several Indian scouts. He prayed that the Lord would continue to give him safe passage.

Revel also knew that Jack Singleton was somewhere behind him, which kept his nerves on edge. What Revel did *not* know was that his riding strategy had put him four days ahead of Singleton.

Revel's strategy was to begin each day's ride at 4:00am. The early darkness made the ride slow and treacherous, but each morning's sunrise gave him the opportunity to run his horse hard in short bursts.

He held the Appaloosa back over hilly, rough terrain, but pushed her hard across every expansive plain. He would be, many times throughout the day, both tortoise and rabbit.

"Easy girl," he spoke softly to his horse under the moonlight. Revel was going through his evening routine, methodically checking her hooves and legs. He frisked each leg searching for burrs and sores. Revel then spent a half hour applying oils to her back, sides, and any small cuts on her legs.

The gift of oils from the Shawnokwans were unlike anything he had ever used. They were highly effective, and the smells differed: peppermint, cinnamon, lavender, eucalyptus, sage, and thyme.

The oil he now applied to his horse smelled like a mixture of mint and kerosene. It seemed to quickly heal her abrasions caused by traveling through chaparrals. It also seemed to keep most of the bugs away from her.

Additionally, his saddle pad, also crafted by the Shawnokwans, was made of a thick layer of sheep's wool with a top-coat of hand-stitched multi-colored fabric. This material went under her flank straps in the same manner, providing comfort to her sides and under-belly.

"Good girl," he encouraged her as he applied the last bit of oil to her rear legs. "We'll be home soon," he said while gently patting her hind quarters.

Revel extinguished his Dakota fire pit and checked his pocket watch. 8:55pm. A Dakota fire pit was an ingenious survival strategy. It consisted of digging two round holes six inches wide by twelve inches deep. The holes were separated by a few inches, so they were very close together. A small horizontal tunnel was opened at the bottom of the holes connecting them together.

The wood for the fire was put into one hole while the other hole remained empty. The design allowed for air to be pulled from the empty hole, acting as a type of vacuum for the fire in the adjascent hole.

The Dakota fire pit offered Revel several crucial benefits: it was virtually smokeless, the flame was undetectable by anyone in the area, it burned fast and hot, and no evidence of a fire remained once the holes were refilled with dirt.

Revel allowed the fire to burn for a strict time limit of thirty minutes. His survival depended upon constant self-discipline.

He laid in the dark replaying the killing of Bristol Singleton in his mind. Even though he had killed Bristol in self-defense, Arthur Meade's reaction had forced him to run.

A few seconds before drifting into sleep, two items remained in his mind: the key and the notebook.

Chapter 21

Jack Singleton rode slowly through a grove of English Oaks and Hard Maples, examining branches. He felt weak and dehydrated.

"*That's the one*," he thought to himself and guided his horse slightly to the right. Jack slipped his boots backwards out of the stirrups as he approached the long horizontal branch of a Silver Maple, slowing his horse.

At just the right moment he reached up and grabbed the large branch, wrapping his arms around the limb. As his horse continued forward, Jack lifted himself upward and out of his saddle.

This maneuver took most of his remaining strength. He swung his feet up around the limb of the tree and worked himself to the top of the branch.

Jack climbed two branches higher trying to find the perfect spot. His horse came to a halt about fifty paces up the trail.

Jack worked to control his breathing as he balanced himself on the tree limb. Sweat rolled down his temples.

"*Betrayal* (he thought to himself) *is an expensive proposition and I have been obliged to waste more time than I can afford.*"

The past three and a half weeks of strenuous tracking had been a challenge for Jack, but he was still on Revel's trail.

A mountain lion had almost gotten to his horse late one evening, forcing him to shoot it with his rifle. He killed two Arapaho scouts who surprised him on the trail and he had spent five days of the journey fighting fever and diarrhea. Those five days had put him behind.

"*Everything changes today.*" The thought made Jack smile as he heard noise on the trail behind. He crouched on the branch staying perfectly still.

"*Wait… wait… wait… now!*" Jack jumped from the branch hitting the rider's shoulder with his boot, resulting in a loud snap: Jack broke the rider's collarbone. The impact blew the rider out of his saddle onto the ground to the right side of the horse. The horse neighed loudly and bolted forward, coming to a stop close to Jack's horse up the trail.

Singleton lay on the ground to the left of the man, trying to recover from the breath being knocked out of him. He watched the other man writhing on the ground, moaning and groping at his shoulder.

Jack, through great effort, managed to get to his feet. He pulled his Colt from his holster and staggered toward the man on the ground.

The man rolled over and saw Jack coming at him. He reached for his gun, but it was too late. Jack kicked him in the face…

Samuel Underwood awoke from unconsciousness to horrible pain in his cheek and shoulder. He had been hog-tied and pulled to the center of the trail. Singleton was squatting next to him. Samuel saw his horse standing next to Jack's horse far up the path.

"Your name, sir?" Jack asked.

"Underwood. Samuel Underwood," he blurted through pain.

Underwood saw that Jack had gotten into his saddlebags, and was now eating Underwood's jerky and drinking from Underwood's canteen.

"Mr. Underwood, why have you been following me?"

"I ain't been following you–"

Underwood's words were interrupted by a fierce punch to his mouth. Samuel fought the pain as he clung to consciousness. Jack took another bite of jerky and continued to talk through chewing.

"Mr. Underwood, I am a man out of time. I have pressing matters to attend to, so I will, benevolently, ask you one last time," said Jack as he dangled his Colt between his knees.

Underwood knew Jack would kill him without hesitation.

"Arthur Meade," admitted Underwood. "He hired me."

"And you are employed by Mr. Meade for what purpose?" Jack asked as he stared into Underwood's blood-shot eyes.

"Mr. Meade contracted me to find you and to verify your movements," Samuel responded honestly.

Jack mulled over Samuel's response. He rose up from his squatted position, holstered his gun and took long drinks of water from Underwood's canteen. Then Jack rolled a cigarette.

"Mr. Underwood," Jack said without looking at Samuel. "Did Mr. Meade hire you to kill me?"

"No, no, no," Underwood replied quickly. The pain in his shoulder and neck were almost unbearable. "He said I just needed to watch you and report back to him–"

"So," Jack interrupted, striking a match and lighting his cigarette. "You are nothing more than a… monitor?" Jack asked as he squatted back down next to Underwood.

"That's all I am. Yes, sir. Just a monitor," Samuel agreed with as much enthusiasm as he could muster, but his body began to tremble with fear as he looked at Jack's face.

Jack took a drag from his cigarette and studied Underwood's eyes. *"Liar,"* Jack said in his mind.

"I believe you, Mr. Underwood," Jack responded with a grin. Samuel felt instant relief.

"If I release you," said Singleton, "Will you go in an opposing direction *and* forget me entirely?"

"Yes, yes – you will never again occupy my thoughts," Underwood replied as his relief intensified.

Jack pulled out his knife and cut the ropes that bound Underwood's wrists and ankles.

"Get yourself up. Get on your horse and do not look back!" Jack commanded.

Underwood, with tremendous strain, managed to get himself into a standing position while fighting the pain and feelings of nausea. He took a cautious look at Jack, then turned up the trial toward his horse.

A thunderous explosion filled the forest. Samuel Underwood's body fell to the ground in a lifeless heap.

Jack holstered his gun, walked over to Underwood's body, and squatted down. He rifled through Underwood's pockets.

"I deem this as self-defense, Mr. Underwood," Jack said to Samuel's dead body. He tied Underwood's Quarter horse to his own horse and thought about his next move.

Knox was somewhere out in front of him, but at this point it didn't matter to Jack. *"Knox is headed home,"* he thought to himself as he tied Underwood's horse to his own.

Jack kicked his black Stallion. The horse responded by lurching forward into a fast trot. He whipped the horse until both were running at peak speed.

Jack rode toward Dodge City, no longer following Revel Knox. The city had a Western Union Telegraph office.

Chapter <u>22</u>

Arthur Meade gazed out into the darkness through the hotel's French windows.

"Honey?" Isabel said from the bed. Arthur turned toward her.

"What is it, Isabel?"

"What are you doing? Why are you not in our bed?" she implored.

"I am thinking. Please go back to sleep."

Isabel flopped over and yanked the covers up to her neck.

Arthur continued to stare out the window. He was nervous.

"*It's been over a month.*" He thought to himself. "*Not a word from Underwood or Singleton. I'm blind.*" Arthur cursed in his mind.

"*Underwood is the best tracker money can buy. He's got to have information on Singleton. Why has Singleton gone rogue? Why hasn't he telegraphed for his weekly expense money? Maybe Singleton caught up to Knox and Knox killed him. No. Can't be. Underwood would have notified me."*

The suppositions and possibilities seemed endless. He walked through the darkness to a small table in his hotel room and poured brandy into a glass tumbler.

Arthur took a drink and listened to Isabel's heavy breathing. She was fast asleep.

"Money and security," he thought as he listened to Isabel's long, sleep-induced breaths. *"She doesn't care for me… she wants my money."*

Meade struck a match and lit the hurricane lamp on the liquor table, lighting up the room. He turned the lamp-wheel counterclockwise to reduce the size of the flame and the illumination of the room. Isabel didn't wake up.

He then lifted his leather satchel from under the table and sat it in the side chair. Arthur retrieved a cigar, snapped off the end with a cigar cutter, removed the globe from the lamp and puffed on the cigar over the flame.

Meade, with a glass of liquor, a fine cigar, and his mistress in his bed, pulled a large stack of documents from his satchel. Each paper was a Contract for Deed, and he held over 200 contracts in the satchel.

"*Vanderkamp, Straussmeyer, Kruger, Richter, Hahn, Gunther, Vanmeter...*" Arthur read the names of the German immigrants on each document.

"*Vanmeter!*" He paused on the name. "*Vanmeter is next.*" Arthur pulled a notepad from the satchel and began to draft ideas for his next victim.

Meade's scheme had put hundreds of thousands of dollars into his pockets. It was an elaborate plan that involved unsuspecting German immigrants moving to Jefferson City to become vineyard husbandmen.

Arthur owned several thousand "Rhineland" acres that he would sell to German immigrants via Contract for Deed. The immigrants would pay a large down-payment for a specific plot of land and sign

Meade's Contract for Deed with great hopesof achieving the American dream.

His contracts specified a monthly "mortgage" payment to be paid in cash. The contracts had a specific clause: in the event of their death, departure, abandonment, or a single late payment, the property would automatically default back to Meade's possession without refund or legal recourse.

Arthur had spent the past twelve years selling vineyards, allowing him to pocket huge down-payments and monthly mortgages. Arthur would then select an underperforming vineyard, kill the family using a variety of tactics, re-acquire the property and sell it to another unsuspecting immigrant family.

Some died in house fires. Some were found in ponds or creeks, as though they had drowned. Some would, through Arthur's position on the Old Dominion Bank Board, find that Arthur had intentionally recorded their mortgage payment a day late, giving Arthur the legal authority to take back the property. Meade was a ruthless and heartless landlord.

However, Arthur had realized many years ago that he needed someone who would kill and burn. He needed someone who had the nerve to do this type of work. He needed someone dependable, greedy, and vicious. That *someone* had been Bristol Singleton, Jack Singleton's brother.

Bristol's death had been a huge blow to Arthur's operation. Arthur couldn't be the one to injure or kill the immigrants. He couldn't be caught setting fire to their homes.

His only option was to take their cash mortgage payments and record the payments as late, causing an automatic repossession and foreclosure of their farms.

Before the death of Bristol, Arthur's scheme had worked successfully for over a decade. The income from his scheme created great wealth for him, but his right-hand man and muscle, Bristol Singleton, was now dead.

"*I'll process Vanmeter's monthly cash mortgage payment two days after the due date,*" Arthur thought to himself as he puffed on the cigar.

"I'll resell that farm in seventy-two hours."

Meade sat in an upholstered wing-back chair next to the small table. He mentally counted his riches while puffing on his fine cigar. He now had enough money and no longer needed to kill.

A notebook lay quietly in a locked strongbox at an unknown location. It was the notebook that Arthur Meade had found out about after Bristol's death, and Arthur's entire life depended upon his ability to find and retrieve it. Who was the author of the notebook? Bristol Singleton.

Bristol had documented every unlawful act he had ever committed for Arthur Meade, along with dates, names, descriptions of Meade's orders, detailed notes of how each crime was committed, and the exact amount of each payment for the commission of every crime – casj payments padi to him by Meade.

Bristol Singleton created and maintained the notebook for one reason… insurance. Bristol's back-up plan had been simple: use the notebook for a plea-deal if he was ever caught in his criminal activities commissioned by Arthur Meade. Bristol never got the chance…

Chapter 23

The theatre company performed an exquisite play. It was a performance being enjoyed by Arthur and his wife, Abigail. They occupied VIP seating in the upper gallery.

A woman leaned over Meade's shoulder and whispered into his ear, "I apologize, Mr. Meade, but you have an urgent telegram from a Mr. Jack Singleton."

Meade offered his apologies to his wife and exited the gallery quickly into the upper hall.

"When did it arrive?" Meade asked Ms. Townsend.

"Thirty minutes ago, sir," she replied.

He took the telegram from her hand. "You're excused, Ms. Townsend," said Arthur. His secretary turned immediately toward the staircase and left the building.

Arthur opened the telegram:

Revel Knox turned south
toward Oklahoma territory,
stop. Will kill him at
Kansas/Oklahoma border,
stop.

Wire check for all
previous week's salaries
a.s.a.p. to Dodge City,
Kansas Western Union
Office, stop.

Confirm $10,000.00 bonus
for Knox's body, stop.

Jack Singleton

Arthur ripped the telegram into small pieces
and threw it into the hallway trash receptacle. He
hurried down the staircase that led into the theatre's
large rotunda and left the theatre toward Jefferson
City's Western Union office.

Meade calculated the total amount and handed the check to the telegraph agent with written instructions.

"*Underwood has betrayed me,*" thought Arthur. "*And Singleton is deceiving me, as well. This will be the last check to Jack Singleton.*" The clerk handed Arthur his receipt.

Arthur stepped out of the telegraph office and looked up at the night sky. "Samuel Underwood, where are you?" he asked the sky in frustration.

Chapter 24

Revel Knox sat very still in his saddle. He was now in the eastern hills of Kansas, approximately twenty miles due south of Topeka.

A band of five renegade Cherokees had formed a circle around him. They each sat on their respective horses, pointing rifles at Revel.

"*Cherokees shouldn't be in this part of Kansas*," Revel thought. "*Be calm.*"

One of the Cherokee riders sidled up to Knox's horse to examine his belongings. Millie had taught a few Shawnokwan phrases to Revel, along with a few words of the Arapaho language. It wouldn't hurt to give it a try.

"*Pe no wakna sho shaw a nay,*" Revel struggled with the words. The Cherokee men looked at one another in confusion.

"*Well, they don't speak Shawnokwan. Maybe I'll try a little Arapaho,*" he thought to himself.

"Uh… *Hini woxhoox nihtokooxuuseet boone*," Revel said as he looked at the Cherokee leader's horse. The men laughed loudly and lowered their rifles.

Revel had tried to say, in Arapaho, "That is a fine horse!" He had, instead, said, "Your horse looks delicious!"

Evidently these Cherokees knew a little Arapaho. Their laughter caused Revel to grin mildly. *"What did I just say?"* he wondered.

The leader of the group vaulted off of his horse and walked to Revel's side. Revel remained very still in the saddle.

The Cherokee examined the piece of saddle blanket that protruded from the rear of the saddle.

"Arapaho?" The leader looked up at Revel as he rubbed the edge of the saddle pad. His tone conveyed a question.

"Wohei," Revel answered. The word meant "yes."

The Cherokee leader stepped back and looked at Revel's eyes. *"Anagisdi osda adanedi,"* replied the Cherokee leader. Translated: Go good spirit.

The Cherokee then turned, ran four steps and leaped onto his horse. The five turned their horses in unison and rode down the hillside through the trees.

The tension of the moment combined with the confusion of what had just happened caused Revel to burst out in laughter. After a moment he sighed with relief.

"I think I just told them that there were a bunch of beautiful women waiting on them at the bottom of this hill," he said to his horse as he patted her neck and laughed. "Let's get out of here while the gettin's good." He kicked his Appaloosa and she started forward down the trail.

Revel smiled in the thought, *"Millie has saved me… again!"*

Chapter <u>25</u>

Dodge City was vibrant with activity. Jack received his check from Arthur Meade at the Western Union office and headed in the direction of the US Calvary post on the east side of town.

He walked confidently through the crowded porches of local businesses and shops as he considered his new plan of action. A stage coach rolled down the dirt street. Cattle-drivers whistled and hollered. Piano music echoed from a saloon across the way. The smell of steak flowed from the doorway of a restaurant and two men, engaged in a fist-fight, hurled punches as he passed.

"*I like this town!*" Jack thought to himself as he walked toward the post. His pace came to an abrupt stop at the Long Branch Saloon's doors, just a few feet in front of Jack – doors bursted open by a man being thrown from the saloon and into the mud and dung of the dirt street.

A finely dressed, slenderly-built man came out of the saloon a step behind the man, pulled his revolver, and focused the barrel on the man in the street.

"Card-cheats ain't welcome in the Long Branch," said the man in a matter-of-fact tone, then shot the cheater in the forehead.

The shot stalled the street's activity, but only for a brief second. Another drunken cheater had just been executed in the dirt, but after that brief moment the populous of Dodge City continued about their business.

"*Yes*," Jack thought as he stepped around the gunfighter and continued his walk toward the Calvary's outpost.

"*This is my kind of place. This might be a spot for a homestead without boredom,*" he thought.

Jack Singleton looked toward the Marshal's office and nodded to Sherriff Charlie Bassett.

Bassett, formerly enlisted in the Union Army at Frankford, Pennsylvania, had been a private in

Company I of the 213th Pennsylvania Infantry. After Lee's surrender, Basset had mustered out in 1865.

It was now October, 1877. Charlie Bassett had drifted throughout the west from 1865 to 1873 working at various jobs in mining, bartending, and buffalo hunting. He had opened the Long Branch Saloon with with Alfred Peacock, but had since sold the saloon.

Charles E. Bassett had been elected as the county sherriff of Ford County in '73, headquartered in Dodge City. Charlie had been elected twice, and was now running for his third term against Bat Masterson, although Kansas was considering a new law preventing Sherriffs from serving three terms. The law would be passed and Masterson would win the election in the next month.

Charlie also served as an assistant city Marshal under his brother, Ed Masterson. James and Wyatt Earp had arrived in Dodge City the previous year.

Bassett eyed Jack Singleton in return as he stood under the porch of the agency.

Jack arrived at the designated US Calvary Registration Tent.

"I am US Marshal Jack Singleton," Jack flashed the badge that he had not returned to the Marshal's office at the time of his resignation.

"How can we be of service, Marshal?" asked the young lieutenant.

"My orders involve tracking a wanted fugitive, and I require arrangements for the utilization of stationed transportation from here to Jefferson City, Missouri."

"Stationed transportation" was a phrase used for horses that could be ran hard from one Calvary outpost to the next. The exhausted horse would be taken to the livery and traded for a fresh horse at each post, thus affording the authorized rider the quickest possible mode of transportation across the country.

The lieutenant opened a large, hard-back journal while retrieving a new invention: a fountain pen. He looked up at Jack.

"The fugitive's name, sir?"

"Revel Knox," replied Jack.

"Your name again, sir?"

"Jack Nickolas Singleton," Jack replied.

"Your superior officer?" Asked the lieutenant as he looked up at Jack.

"Arthur Meade," Jack spelled out Arthur's last name.

"Excellent," said the young Calvary soldier. He pulled a piece of blank paper from a shelf with the US Calvary's official insignia on the letterhead, scribbled a message in the blank body of the paper, signed it and slammed it with a metal stamp.

"Sir, show this document at each post and you will be provided with a fresh horse ready for travel. Now, if you will accompany me, we will ready you at the livery."

Singleton folded the document and inserted it into his inner vest pocket. The two men stepped into the large livery stable. Mexicans hurried around the stables taking care of the many duties created by the growing population of Dodge City.

Jack turned to the lieutenant and grabbed his arm. "Young man, you see that large black stallion in stall number three?"

The young man scanned the stalls, found number three and replied, "Yes, sir."

"That is one of the finest of its breed and it is *my* horse," Jack's eyes seemed to burn holes through the young soldier.

"And do you see that Quarter horse in pen seven?" Jack asked.

"Yes, sir," replied the young soldier.

Jack pulled a gold coin from his vest pocket and placed it into the hand of the lieutenant. "That Quarter horse is now *yours*," Jack said with a grin.

The young man peered at the gold coin in the palm of his hand, then slowly looked up at Jack.

"But, sir–"

"Son," Jack interrupted. "Today you have been gifted a fine Quarter horse, the saddle and gear that came with it, and gold worth about three months of your salary. Consider these gifts compliments of the US Marshal Service."

The young soldier's mouth dropped open slightly. He shook his head in the affirmative, continuing to hang on every syllable uttered by Singleton.

"Thank you, sir–"

"The mission that I am on," Jack interrupted again, "is classified and cannot be discussed with anyone. Do you understand me?"

"Yes," the soldier shook his head eagerly. "Yes, sir. Absolutely, sir! You have my word as a representative of the US Calvary. Your mission will remain confidential in my utmost care and trust." The lieutenant snapped his boots together as if coming to attention. He followed with a precise salute to Jack Singleton.

Singleton fought back a laugh.

"Now, lieutenant, show me my station horse."

"Sir, please remain here for a moment." The young man found the livery operator, said something to him that Jack couldn't make out, pointed to Jack, then walked quickly back.

"Our livery stableman is ready to speak to you, sir," said the soldier.

"Thank you for your expedient service, young man. And remember, this is a classified operation," Jack said to the young man as he narrowed his eyes.

"You are welcome, sir. I am happy to be of service to a representative of these glorious United States. Sir, your mission will be maintained within the most strict of personal discipline." He saluted Jack a second time and left the stables quickly.

Jack turned to the livery operator who escorted him to pen number sixteen.

"She'll run pretty hard for 'bout ten miles. Just don't kill 'er before you get to the next post. Use your transfer stamp to process her in and get you a fresh horse." The livery operator spoke the instructions in a monotone voice without any emotion or concern.

Jack's plan was working. He examined the horse as the livery operator waited a few feet from the pen.

"What is your name?" asked Jack.

"Albert Bennett," replied the livery operator.

"My name is Marshal Jack Singleton," Jack introduced himself while pulling out three gold coins. Gold he had taken from Samuel Underwood's dead body.

Albert extended his hand expecting a handshake from Jack. Jack, instead, placed the gold coins into Albert's dirty hand.

"Mr. Bennett, that Stallion in pen number three means the world to me. I expect your undying attention and service to my horse. Let nothing happen to him. He had better be in the same excellent condition on the day of my return as you find him currently.

"I will return within the next few months. This should be more than enough to insure that my stallion receives your utmost attention during this time period."

Bennett smiled. "Mister," Bennett cursed as he looked at the gold in his hand, "For this much gold I'll sleep in that stall with your horse!"

"Good enough," Jack said and turned toward the horse he was about to mount. "I'll see you in a few months."

"And, Mr. Bennett," Jack turned back to Bennett. "If, upon my return, that Stallion is not in the best condition, I will put three loads of lead into your skull to match those three gold coins in your filthy hand."

"You ain't got nothing to worry about, Marshal Singleton," Albert looked at Jack with a tremor of fear. Jack squatted and tied spurs to his boots.

Albert held the reigns of the mustang as Jack mounted the horse. Singleton took the reins and nodded to Albert Bennett. He pushed the spurs into the Mustang's sides and that was more than enough – the Mustang bolted from the entrance of the livery and Jack fought to hang on. He hated Mustangs.

As Jack's new horse exceled beyond the edge of Dodge City, he felt like a young man again.

"*Close the gap!*" Singleton hollered and cursed at the horse as he leaned forward. He had forgotten the thrill of riding a horse of this speed and nature.

"Revel Knox, I'm coming for you!" he screamed into the wind.

Chapter <u>26</u>

Arthur Meade had just finished his closing arguments and the defense lawyer stood to address the jury.

One of Arthur's clients, a local cattleman, was suing another cattleman over a free-range land dispute.

The defense attorney was a weak young man fresh out of law school. Meade only half-listened to the defense attorney's closing remarks. He had already won the case. Fatigue and a lack of sleep were showing on Arthur's face. His thoughts drifted…

Isabel, Underwood, Singleton, Knox, the notebook."

"Mr. Meade," said the judge. Arthur gazed across the room.

"Mr. Meade!" the judge's loud voice jolted Arthur back to reality.

"Yes, your honor," Meade's body jerked as he was caught off guard.

"Councilor, do you require a nap?" The judge's sarcasm caused laughs from the gallery.

"I apologize, your honor." Meade did his best to seem humble.

"Our gracious jurors will reconvene tomorrow morning providing you agree to the consumption of a pot of coffee prior to our engagement," quipped the judge, followed by another round of laughs from the gallery.

"More than suitable, your honor, and I promise to retire early this evening," Meade replied as the courtroom stood.

"Wake up," Arthur's client whispered to him through clinched teeth. "I am paying you a lot of money–"

"Mr. Steed," Arthur interrupted in a return whisper. "You have paid me to win and that is exactly what I have done for you." He retrieved his satchel and walked away from the large courtroom table without looking back at his client.

Ms. Townsend opened Arthur's office door slowly and poked her head through. He sat at his desk rubbing his eyes with the palms of his hands. She looked at his desk. Smoke from his burning cigar rose upward as a silver string and she saw the short tumbler full of liquor.

"Mr. Meade?"

Arthur quickly pulled his palms from his eyes and stood up behind his desk.

"What is it, Ms. Townsend?"

"We have just received a telegram that is sealed," she said as she brought the envelope to his desk. "It is marked FYEO (for your eyes only)."

Arthur thanked Ms. Townsend and dismissed her. He waited until she exited and closed his office door.

Meade removed a letter opener from his center desk drawer and slid it through the edge of the envelope, pulled out the telegram and dropped the envelope into the trash can next to his desk. The telegram said:

> `Revel Knox spotted south of Kansas City, Missouri, stop.`

```
Thought you would want to
know, stop.

A Friend from KC, MO
```

"Ah–!" Meade shouted a curse word so loud that Ms. Townsend, in the outer office, jumped in her chair.

He read the document three times finding the date and time stamp, but no name. Arthur then grabbed the envelope from the trash can. The front contained the Western Union insignia and their Kansas City return address, Meade's Law office address, and ⊦Υ◯Ε scribbled on the back below the seal.

He threw the telegram to the floor and sat down hard in his expensive leather office chair. He scanned the names of his contacts in Kansas City, but no one came to mind.

"It doesn't matter who sent it. I've got bigger fish to fry right now. Revel is coming back! Underwood and Singleton have failed me," thought

Meade. *"I'll deal with this a different way!"* Arthur grabbed his suitcoat and hurried to the US Marshal's office.

"I don't care about your resources or how many men it's going to take!" Arthur screamed at the Marshal while stepping toward his desk.

"Mr. Meade, we simply cannot send every resource we have to intercept one man," the marshal pled.

Meade narrowed his eyes and spoke in a tone just louder than a whisper, "If I go down, you will go down with me. Understand?"

"I understand–"

"Then get it done," Arthur interrupted. "Immediately!" He shouted as he turned and stomped out of the marshal's office.

The marshal dispatched seventeen companies of men with three in each company. It was the largest deployment of manpower in the city's history, and represented every type of available lawman in Cole County.

The teams were gathered together around the Rhineland Park Gazebo. A young boy handed each team a sketch and description of Revel Knox.

"Gentlemen, Knox is highly dangerous. Many of you know him and you know that he murdered Bristol Singleton and Edward Crab in cold blood," Meade announced to the large group. "He injured Collin Phelps. We have reason to believe he has killed others, which is why I will pay the man who kills him a $12,000.00 reward, in cash, upon delivery of his dead body!"

Excited chatter spread through the crowd.

"Wait, wait," Meade held up both hands. "In addition, Revel Knox is in possession of highly classified government documents that are not to be examined, but returned to me immediately upon arrival.

"Therefore," continued Arthur, "I will provide an additional $10,000.00 cash bonus for the safe return of those documents." The men could hardly contain their enthusiasm.

"However, any man who reads the documents in Knox's possession will be considered a treasonous individual and will be hanged from the neck until dead. Do you understand?" The group indicated that they understood his instructions.

"Now go get him!" Arthur yelled.

The teams raced to their horses and mounted up. They spread from Jefferson City in a fanlike pattern, traveling southwest, west and northwest.

Arthur Meade watched the men as they rode out of sight. He felt a sense of relief and hope.

Chapter <u>27</u>

Elizabeth Knox sat at the kitchen table in her elegant, two-story home: one of the finer homes in all of Cole County. The home had been purchased for her by her brother, Revel, a few years prior.

She was all that remained of Revel's family. Elizabeth read the telegram that contained four simple words:

It is time, stop.

A chill swept over her body followed by goose-bumps on her arms.

She held the tip of the telegram over the flame of the candle on the table. Her hand was shaking.

She then stood and walked carefully to the cook-stove as the paper began to flame, opened the wood-box door, placed the burning telegram inside, and closed the door.

Elizabeth then went into her large living room. Light from the evening's dusk came through the west side's large plantation-style windows, slightly illuminating the space. Victorian furniture was positioned around the palatial fireplace and a wide, cherry-railed staircase opened at the opposite side.

She knelt down on her knees and removed all of the books from the bottom shelf of the custom-built bookcase underneath the stairs, exposing the end of a pencil-sized dowel rod protruding from the back of the shelf.

Elizabeth pulled on the rod releasing a small wooden door at the rear of the shelf. The door was nine inches tall by eighteen inches wide.

She opened the door and stared inside… there was the metal strongbox that held Bristol Singleton's notebook. It was a box that had a lock on each end.

Opening the box required two different keys. The two keys had to be inserted into the locks and turned simultaneously to open the lid.

Her thoughts went back to the morning after Revel had fled Jefferson City. The town Marshal and his deputies had shown up at her door with a search warrant.

The men had searched her large home, but had reluctantly given up after three hours, not finding the document Meade had demanded they find.

Elizabeth pulled the metal strongbox from the hidden space and took it to her upstairs bedroom closet.

One key had been inserted into a one of the box's locks… the other lock remained empty.

Chapter 28

Revel was a few days from Jefferson City, Missouri. The late evening sun was at his back and his Appaloosa carried him at a quick gate through a field of wild flowers.

He saw a flash several hundred yards out in front of him: three riders coming toward his position.

Revel quickly turned his horse to the left through a thick tree line and down into a steep ravine. He stopped her in the dry creek-bed at the bottom and jumped from the saddle.

Revel fought to climb back up the steep embankment on foot. After managing to get to the top, he laid down flat on his stomach and crawled to the edge of the tree line. Revel removed his hat and drew the Cooper from his holster.

The riders rode quickly past his position, but slow enough for him to see their badges. He also recognized one of the three men and smiled.

"The sun was in their eyes – that's why they didn't see me," he thought. Revel eased back down the ravine to his horse.

"We'll spend the night right here, girl," he spoke softly to the Appaloosa and stroked the side of her neck.

Revel took a knee and thanked God for His love, mercy and grace. He thanked God for Jesus Christ and prayed for wisdom.

Revel closed the prayer, stood up and bit off a piece of chewing tobacco from his saddlebag, then sat down on the ground by his horse.

He looked up at her and she seemed to look back at him. "God is with us, girl," Revel talked to his horse as if she were a person.

"Sure feels odd," he thought as he rubbed his bare cheeks with his fingers.

He had, the day before, come upon a stage coach that had stopped to water their horses. The man riding shot-gun traded Revel a straight razor for one of Revel's Shawnokwan skinning knives.

Revel was now unrecognizable. He was twenty-five pounds lighter than he had been when he'd fled Jefferson City: strong and lean.

After wearing a beard for almost ten years, his face was now clean shaven, revealing a small scar on his left cheek. He had also used the straight razor to cut off his long hair to a short-cropped style.

Revel looked like a totally different person, which was his plan.

"*I'm going to ride this Appaloosa right through the middle of Jefferson City,*" he thought with a smile.

Chapter 29

Jack Singleton had almost killed six of the many Mustangs used throughout his trip. It was dark and he was filling out paperwork at Jefferson City's Calvary Post.

"Where is everyone?" asked Singleton.

"On some kind of manhunt. Left a few days ago," said the melancholy private sitting at a desk under the tent.

Jack's eyes narrowed as he looked up at the kid. "Manhunt for *whom*?"

"Somebody named Knox. I don't really know, mister," replied the private without concern.

"I do *not* appreciate the condition of that horse, Mr. Singleton," shouted a young and angry Captain who was approaching Jack at the processing desk.

"How much will it cost?" Jack asked without looking up from his paperwork.

"Do you think you can just–"

Singleton grabbed the young captain by the throat. As the captain tried to break free, Jack reached into his pants pocket with his other hand and pulled out a gold coin.

"Take this and get back to where you came from, boy," Singleton said as he released the man's throat. The captain took the coin with a snap and ran.

"What else has Meade done?" Singleton asked himself.

Jack casually pulled a dark blanket from a neighborhood clothes line as he walked from the edge of town toward the hotel. He flung the blanket around his shoulders concealing his clothing.

"I need a hat," he thought. At that moment a drunk exited the saloon onto the boardwalk and Jack turned instinctively toward him. He quickly crossed the main thoroughfare toward the wobbling man.

Jack's swift uppercut to the man's jaw knocked him out cold. Jack picked up the hat.

He stepped under the porch of the Marshal's Office and ripped a flyer from the public notice board hanging on the outside wall. It was a wanted poster for Revel Knox. Jack shook his head in disbelief of the amounts now offered for Knox.

"*And what is this about Knox carrying a classified government document?*" He questioned in his mind. "*I'll cut out Meade's double-crossing heart!*" He folded and pocketed the paper.

"Need a room for a week," Jack grunted to the hotel desk clerk.

"Yes, sir. Happy to oblige. First or second floor?" the chipper clerk asked.

"Second," Singleton replied while pushing a gold coin across the counter. "And make it facing the thoroughfare."

"Oh, yes sir!" The clerk pocketed the coin. It was the last of the gold coins Jack had taken from Samuel Underwood's dead body.

"And your name, sir?"

Singleton kept his head down as he considered the question.

"Sir, your name please?" the clerk courteously repeated the question.

"My name?" Jack looked up at the clerk. "My name is Revel Knox," Jack said.

"Excellent, Mr. Knox. Here is your key. Room 204." Jack Singleton took the key from the clerk's hand and left him in mid-sentence.

"Mr. Knox, it is a fine room that overlooks Main Street," the clerk said to Jack's back. Singleton kept walking. He went up the staircase, secured the room and extinguished all of the kerosene lamps except the one next to the water pot.

Jack then closed the draperies at each of the four windows. He was exhausted. His legs, back, inner-thighs and rear-end ached severely.

The pot held fresh water. A new bar of lye soap and two clean towels had been placed neatly beside the bowl.

Even though Jack was exhausted, he operated as disciplined men do, never allowing their current feelings to dictate their immediate and necessary actions.

Jack stripped off his clothes, lathered his face, and looked into the mirror. He cursed at his appearance and proceeded to shave off six months' worth of facial hair, stopping just short of his finely waxed handle-bar mustache… his trademark.

"Shave it off, Jack. Shave it off and the plan will work," he said aloud. Jack retrieved a small set of clippers and began working on his mustache.

Five minutes later Jack looked at his reflection. "*No worse for wear*," he thought.

Now 40lbs. lighter, and a completely shaven face, Jack was also unrecognizable.

He, after shaving, worked efficiently in cleaning and preparing his guns in the low light of his hotel room. Jack then placed his most prized possession on the hotel bed and found his sharpening rock. He began sharpening his knife…

Chapter 30

A loud banging sound emanated from the front door.

Arthur Meade jolted from the unconsciousness of sleep and checked his watch. 5:01am.

"*This better be good*," Arthur thought as he opened the front door.

"Mr. Meade," the young cattleman stood at the doorway. "I apologize for disturbing you at such an–"

"Just get to it!" exclaimed Arthur.

"Word from the US Calvary Post. A captain said that Jack Singleton got into town last night," the man said and turned to leave.

Arthur slowly closed the door. He felt his blood turn to ice.

Twenty minutes later he was dressed and on his way to Isabel's home.

"Get dressed and pack your things," Arthur blurted at her as he came through her back door.

"What is it? What has happened–"

"Isabel," Arthur grabbed both of her arms. "We have not the time to discuss the details. We must enact our plan immediately. You will be on the early morning stagecoach toward Wilmington," he released her shoulders and went to her bedroom.

"Arthur, please! We planned to go together," she whined in protest.

"Isabel," he said as he stopped and turned. "We are in great danger!"

Isabel put her hand to her mouth in fear.

"A man arrived in town last night. If I do not take care of him he will track us, find us, and kill us both," Arthur said dramatically. His acting skills were better than hers.

"Take the coach and let me deal with this issue. I will meet you at the port in North Carolina in three weeks."

She tried to cry but couldn't fabricate the tears.

"And, sweetheart," Arthur continued, "Here is enough cash to keep you well for three weeks. I will arrive with the rest and we will sail away from Wilmington, never to look back."

She clutched him tightly. "My dear, Arthur. I will be lost without you. Please know that my heart is yours," she said in her thick Spanish accent.

Isabel lifted her head and looked into his eyes. "Promise me. Three weeks."

Meade smiled and kissed her cheek. "Three weeks, my love."

An hour later, Isabel sat in the east-bound stagecoach. Arthur closed the coach door. She waved and smiled as the coach pulled away.

Arthur stood at the edge of Main Street and waved goodbye to Isabel.

"Good riddance you money-grubbing whore," Arthur said under his breath as he waved. "*Stranded, alone, and broke in Wilmington,*" Arthur thought to himself. He laughed, unable to contain his relief.

Arthur's feelings for Isabel had died when he realized that he was nothing more to her than an aging tycoon.

Arthur was now rid of her monthly stipend. Better yet, *all* of the money would be his and his alone.

"Adios, Amiga!" he said as he walked briskly toward his law office. The porches of the connecting shops covered the boarded sidewalk. It was already filled with people.

"Pardon me," Arthur said to a man that had bumped into him so hard that he was almost knocked off of the boardwalk. Arthur caught his balance, looked at the man, and continued a fast pace to his office.

Jack Singleton smiled without returning a "Pardon me" or an apology for bumping Arthur intentionally. He watched Arthur's round body bob down the walkway. Jack loved this part of the chase…

Chapter 31

Revel had spent the previous night in a large, well-equipped vineyard barn; a barn Revel owned. It sat on the south-side of his 2000-acre plot.

Even though the location was strategic, he couldn't allow himself to stay in any one location for more than a night.

Revel left the barn and arrived in town before sunrise. His Appaloosa swung her head up and down, pulling at the reigns tied to Old Dominion Bank's hitching post.

He took a bite from a Granny Smith apple as he sat comfortably in a rocking chair positioned under the canopy of Old Dominion.

Revel Knox wore an expensive, custom-tailored business suit accompanied by a bold red tie and black wingtip shoes: clothing previously retrieved from his ward-robe at Elizabeth's home.

He stood from the rocker looking back and forth at two men: Arthur Meade and Jack Singleton.

Meade's movements were easy and predictable, but Singleton? Revel had gotten lucky… or maybe it had been the providence of God.

Revel, only one hour earlier, had been looking for the print along Jefferson City's main thoroughfare and he had found it. It was Jack's boot print.

Jack Singleton wore a rare and very expensive pair of riding boots that could only be obtained in New York City. The cost of these specific boots were approximately six times the cost of any other high quality pair of boots.

Jack's wealthy father had taught him to spend exorbitant amounts of money on two things: boots and mattresses. Why? Because a man spends a lot of time in both; however, in Jack's line of work he had opted for boots and guns.

Revel had seen the boot-print many times throughout the previous months and knew it well. All he had to do now was to follow the prints. They had led to the Drake Hotel and also to the backside of Meade's office.

After finding the prints he found the best vantage point of the Drake Hotel and Arthur's law office. He sat and waited for the boots to exit the Drake.

When he saw the boots come out, Revel didn't recognize the man wearing them. The man was much lighter than Jack Singleton, and he was clean-shaven. No handle-bar mustache.

However, when Singleton looked toward Revel's direction, Revel recognized his eyes. There was no mistake. Jack was using the same *hide-in-the-open* strategy.

Revel tossed the apple core into the street as he watched the two men. Meade entered his law office down the street, disappearing from Revel's sight.

Revel looked back to Jack's position. Jack was now coming directly toward Revel.

Knox casually took his seat in the rocker. When he looked up toward Singleton, now only ten feet away, their eyes locked.

Revel gently moved his arm toward his left inside coat pocket and put his hand around the grip of his concealed Cooper. Revel's other breast pocket held Bristol's notebook previously retrieved from the dual-keyed lock-box at Elizabeth's home.

Jack Singleton's eyes narrowed as he looked into the eyes of Revel Knox. Jack stopped abruptly and put his hand on the grip of his holstered pistol.

"Do I know you?" Jack asked the businessman sitting in the rocker. Uneasiness filled his body. He squeezed the handle of his Colt, ready to draw down on the man.

"*Das macht nichts, narr*," Revel replied in perfect German.

"Germans," Jack grunted with a curse word as he removed his hand from his Colt and walked around Revel into the Old Dominion Bank.

Revel smiled as he removed his hand from his pistol.

Chapter <u>32</u>

Jack presented several months of uncashed checks from Arthur Meade to the teller.

"Good morning, sir," said the young woman across the counter.

"Good morning, mam," replied Jack.

"So," she examined the checks. "These are made out to you from the Hillerbrand Lumber Company of St. Louis?"

"Yes." Jack's reponse was terse.

"I'm going to need to verify the company–"

"No need, mam," Jack interrupted. "The company is owned by Arthur Meade."

"Oh, I see. Well, Mr. Meade is one of our board members. Please forgive me for troubling you," replied the woman with a smile. She counted out the large sum of cash without verifying Hillerbrand Lumber Company.

Jack stood at the teller's window looking out through the bank's large front windows. He watched that German mount an Appaloosa. Something didn't feel right.

"Here you are, sir." Her word's interrupted his thoughts. She handed him a large crème-colored envelope filled with an enormous amount of cash.

"Anything else we can do for you, Mr. Singleton?"

Jack was already walking away, but her question stopped him in his tracks. He thought for just a moment and turned back toward her.

"Yes, mam, there are two things you can do for me," he smiled, stepping close to the bank counter.

"What is that, sir?"

"Call your board members together," he said as his smile disappeared.

"And why would I do that, Mr. Singleton?" she was confused.

"Because Hillerbrand Lumber is a fake company created by Arthur Meade," Singleton said flatly.

The young lady's mouth dropped open and her eyes grew wide.

"And this big bag of money you've just given me…" he paused for effect.

She slowly nodded her head as if to say "yes?"

"This is the bank's money, lady!" Jack said and walked toward the bank's front doors. "And tell Arthur I said hello," he said loudly as he walked out.

Chapter <u>33</u>

Revel kicked the Appaloosa. He rode across the open grassland of his property headed toward one of his many barns.

Upon arrival he walked his horse into the barn and began his evening ritual of inspection and oil application. She loved the attention.

"Good girl," he encouraged her as he frisked each leg.

He finished and stabled her, then pulled off the red tie.

"*God bless you, Elizabeth,*" he said in his mind after seeing the change of clothes, bowl of water, soap and food in the far corner. Revel stripped down to his underwear.

His horse snorted in her pen as he shaved his face.

"Are you upset by our lack of communication?" Revel asked his horse as he tipped his head backward, running the razor in an upward motion from his neck to the edge of his chin. He dipped the razor into the bowl and turned his head toward his horse.

"Because I know that women appreciate a man who communicates with them," Revel stared at the horse. Nothing.

"Alright," he turned back to the water bowl. "Be that way," he said as he continued to shave.

He changed into his cattleman's clothes. The shirt smelled fresh.

He and Elizabeth followed the plan. She had been so good to him and he deeply regretted having put her in such a dangerous position. Revel simply did not have any other options. They were family and they would always give their life for one another.

His thoughts drifted to the salvation offered by Jesus Christ. *"I've got to share this with Elizabeth – she'll be so excited! I know she will obey the gospel!"* He thought as he blew out the candle.

Revel laid back in the comfort of the straw and covered himself with a quilt made by his grandmother.

He thought about the anonymous telegram that he had sent to Meade weeks before. It was the telegram that had informed Arthur Meade of himself "being spotted south of Kansas City."

He thought about how he had ended the telegram… "*A friend from KC, MO.*"

Revel had sent the anonymous telegram to Arthur as a strategy to motivate Meade toward dispatching the county's lawmen. It had worked. The risk of local law enforcement was now minimized.

Revel's mind went to a basic Bible principle. How could he follow Christ's teaching?

> *But love ye your enemies, and do good, and lend, hoping for nothing again; and your reward shall be great, and ye shall be the children of the Highest: for he is kind unto the unthankful and to the evil* (Luke 6:35).

"*Meade is my enemy. How can I love him? How can I do good to that snake?*" The questions looped in Revel's mind until God provided the wisdom that Revel had been praying for: *Don't kill Arthur. Just capture him. Turn him and the notebook over to the authorities. Let God take care of it from there.*

It made perfect sense. He would be honest about the events surrounding Bristol's death and his need to flee. The notebook would help exonerate him and would, most likely, cause Arthur Meade to hang.

Revel's mind was active and sleep was a distant possibility. His thoughts drifted to his past…

Chapter 34

Revel's past was remarkably unique.

His grandparents had helped found Jefferson City. They were proud German immigrants who valued America's principles, her foundation stones, and all that she represented.

They loved the fact that everyone who came to America assimilated into the American culture.

Immigrants from all over the globe relinquished their own cultures, languages, and traditions, embracing everything that was American.

Assimilation didn't mean inferiority – it meant something powerful! Immigrants *voluntarily* assimilated into this new culture: a culture established upon individual freedom, morality, and the opportunity to pursue one's dreams. That was America.

A man or woman could be poor in every territory of the globe; however, America allowed that *same* poor man or woman the opportunity to develop an idea, turn it into something tangible, and build it into something incredible.

The poor in America had something that no other country offered… the opportunity to turn dreams into reality.

Revel thought of the foundation that his grandparents had established and the resources that this region offered the many German immigrants who followed.

Revel was an American with a proud German heritage. His grandfather established the first vineyard in Cole County. He built the first hardware store in Jefferson City and had helped two ambitious businessmen found the Old Dominion Bank.

The wealth that his grandparents had amassed through struggle, sacrifice, and sixteen-hour work-days had been passed down to his parents.

Revel's mother and father had instilled into him the finest morals and prinicples, even though he had abandoned those attributes during his rebellious years.

His father taught him the German language from an early age. He groomed Revel in philosophy, agriculture, literature, agriculture, and business.

At the age of sixteen, Revel was transported to New York City by his parents. It was 1860, and he was to attend New York's prestigious Columbia College, formerly named King's College founded in 1754.

Columbia's alumni touted great men, such as: John Jay, the first Chief Justice of the US, Alexander Hamilton, the first Secretary of the Treasury, Governor Morris, the author of the final draft of the US Constitution, and Robert R. Livingston, a member of the five-man board who that created the Declaration of Independence.

Revel excelled at Columbia, earning dual-degrees in Economics and Agricultural Science.

He returned to Jefferson City after his graduation. The year was 1866 and Revel was twenty-two years old. Both of his parents had died (1864 and 1865, respectively) from Tuberculosis.

He and his sister, Elizabeth, were the sole survivors and heirs of the Knox Estate. Revel had inherited his family's home, their many businesses in Jefferson City, and 3000 acres of prime vineyard ground.

Revel sold the family businesses to the employees of each business, thus creating one of the first conceptual "employee-owned" business models in the state of Missouri.

When Revel sold a business owned by the Knox Estate, he required two conditions within the written contract:

1. The business must donate 2.5% of their yearly net profits to the Jefferson City Library, as long as the business generated a minimum annual net profit of 38%.

2. Secondly, 12% of the business's annual net profits must be

distributed equally among every employee-owner.

Revel donated his deceased parent's home to Jefferson City to be used as the city's primary library. He also utilized the profits from the sales of the many family-owned businesses to build and furnish an elaborate home for his younger sister.

He and Elizabeth had agreed to donate one-third of their inherited acreage to the city's economic development department, with three stipulations:

1. The donated 1000 acres be parceled on the condition that the total acreage would be sub-divided into fifty individual plots consisting of twenty acres in each plot.

2. Each plot would be reserved for a qualified German family for the sole purpose of vineyard husbandry.

3. Each qualifying German family would, subsequently, have a guarantee of financing for

the purpose of building a home and at least one barn on each twenty-acre plot, financed exclusively by Old Dominion Bank at 1% below the current prime lending rate.

Revel's program had been an ingenious economic boon for Jefferson City, Missouri. Fifty qualified German immigrant families were bestowed the 20-acre plots, and each were to keep all of the profits of their own labors.

The bank provided low interest mortgages to each family, with the land used as collateral. Revel's deceased father had been an important board member at Old Dominion before his death, and his parents would have been very proud of Revel and Elizabeth's vision of the future, as well as their generous gifts to the community.

Immigrants came as word spread. Farms were established rapidly and the city flourished.

The Knox Estate had more money than Elizabeth or Revel could spend in *three* life-times, and they still owned, after the donation of the 1000 acres, 2000 acres of premium vineyard land.

However, Revel had grown restless a few months after he and Elizabeth had finalized the management and distribution of their large family estate.

Old Dominion had hired him immediately following his return from Columbia, but working in an office and wearing a tie bored Revel.

After resigning from the bank, Revel volunteered his time working in the vineyards with the various German families, but the vineyards didn't satisfy him, either.

Revel's passion? Cattle. He loved cattle and everything about them. He especially loved driving cattle over long distances. It was a life he hadn't learned at Columbia College.

The cattle-driving lifestyle seemed to call to Revel, so he'd put his degrees in a desk drawer, pushed his cultured character to the back burner, and had spent the past ten years embracing the hard and rough business of cattle-driving. It had been a most challenging adventure of his life.

"I think mom and dad would be proud of me," Revel thought to himself.

"No, they would not be proud. The drunkenness, the brothels, the fist-fights – the trappings of the cowboy lifestyle would have broken their hearts."

Tears formed in his eyes. Even though God had forgiven Revel of his past sins when immersed into Christ*, the regret and shame still haunted his mind and heart… something every good man struggles with.

Revel drifted into sleep.

*1 Peter 3:21; Acts 22:16

Chapter 35

Revel jumped up violently. "It was just a dream," he said aloud to himself. He laid back onto the straw and pulled the blanket away from his sweat-covered body.

"It was just a dream," he repeated.

The dream was about his sister, Elizabeth, and Jack's brother, Bristol.

Revel lay quietly and listened to the wind whistling through the slats of the old barn.

He thought about his altercation with Bristol Singleton, Friday, April 3, 1877 – 6 months ago:

Revel had arrived at Elizabeth's home one afternoon following a four-week cattle-drive. Elizabeth greeted him at the door and what he saw shocked him.

"Did *he* do that to you?" Revel questioned Elizabeth with a mix of shock and anger.

"Don't hurt him, Revel," she begged.

"When did it happen?" asked Revel. His eyes swept over her face and arms.

"Last night," she admitted.

Looking at her bruises and imagining what she had been through the previous evening throttled Revel's anger.

"Where is he now?" Revel asked calmly as he looked into his sister's eyes.

"Revel, please don't hurt him–"

"Elizabeth," interrupted Revel. "Is he coming back here tonight?"

"No," Elizabeth responded quickly. "I told him that I never wanted to see him again," she cried.

Bristol had been courting Elizabeth Knox during the past six weeks: four of which Revel had been away on a cattle drive.

Bristol Singleton was handsome, self-centered, and arrogant. He was also considered to be one of the premier bachelors in Cole County, second only to Revel.

Elizabeth had mistakenly thought that Bristol was a man of character. And, like everyone else in the community, she didn't know about his criminal activities with Arthur Meade.

Bristol, in a drunken rage, had beaten Elizabeth during the previous evening.

Revel put his sister in their wagon, teamed the horses, and took her to Dr. Bledig's home in town.

He had, after bringing her back from the doctor's home, tucked her into her bed.

Revel looked at the large grandfather clock in her bedroom. 4:30pm. He knew Bristol would be at the saloon and he hoped that Bristol, at this time of the afternoon, would not *yet* be drunk.

Revel kicked his horse toward the Vineyard Saloon. He controlled his anger, not wanting to take out his fury on his innocent horse.

Revel found Bristol Singleton's horse at the Vineyard Saloon. He removed his guns, entered the saloon and demanded Bristol to come outside. Bristol followed Revel out of the saloon onto the boardwalk.

"What do you want?" Bristol's cocky attitude only fueled Revel's anger.

"You *know* what I want with you," Revel said as he tempered his anger.

"Oh," Bristol laughed. His body swayed slightly from the alcohol.

"Your little sister," he said as he put his hand on his holstered revolver.

"You are taking up for your little sister! Guess you know about our fight last night," Bristol said sarcastically as he stepped from the boardwalk into the dirt thoroughfare.

"So, she's got a few bruises. No big deal!" Bristol antagonized Revel.

Revel realized that Bristol was drunk and decided it best to wait until Bristol sobered up.

Revel turned away from Bristol and walked toward his horse.

"Don't you turn your back on me!" Bristol screamed. "I'll put a bullet in your head–"

Revel spun quickly and yanked Bristol's pistols from his holsters, disarming Bristol and beating him with the handle of one of the guns.

Revel then cast aside Bristol's guns and pummeled Bristol's face and body with his bare hands.

Bristol lay on his back in the dirt as Revel stood over him. The beaten man looked up at Revel through watery eyes, a blood-covered face, and intense pain.

"If you *ever*," Reveal said as he stood over Bristol, "touch my sister again, I will kill you!" Revel said.

Revel mounted his horse as Bristol passed out.

Chapter 36

[The following evening on Saturday, April 4, 1877 - 6 months ago]:

Revel stood very still as he peered down the barrel of Bristol's long Colt revolver positioned an inch from Revel's nose.

He could smell the liquor on Bristol's breath as Bristol spoke. Revel had been jumped by three men who had beaten him, than had drug him to the rear of the Vineyard Saloon. They were going to kill Revel.

Bristol held the Colt at Revel's face while Edward Crab stood behind Knox holding a shotgun at Revel's back. Collin Phelps stood up the alleyway between the saloon and hardware store, acting as a lookout.

Collin couldn't see his two friends holding Revel, but he could hear bits and pieces of the conversation.

"Don't you know who *I* am?" Bristol loudly asked Revel. "*I* am the brother of the finest US Marshal that has ever lived," he bragged about Jack Singleton as he put the bottle to his lips and tipped it upward. Revel looked into Bristol's blood-shot eyes. Bristol was hammered with liquor and seeking revenge for the beating who received by Revel the previous evening.

"Better than James or Wyatt Earp!" Bristol praised Jack loudly.

"Ed," Bristol called to the man behind Revel. "Tonight we're gonna have a little fun with Elizabeth after I put a hole through his skull," laughed Bristol. He continued to hold the Colt to Revel's face.

"*Be calm and wait for the moment,*" Revel controlled his mind and body. Edward Crab laughed and whooped at Bristol's comment about Elizabeth.

Collin Phelps, the lookout, heard Ed's laughter and howls, causing him to move slowly down the alleyway toward them. He was missing out on all the fun.

"Revel Knox! The great Revel Knox!" yelled Bristol as he wobbled back and forth.

"Let me tell you who else *I* am," bragged Bristol. "*I* am a killer," he slurred his words. "*I* am the scariest man you've ever met!"

"As a matter of fact, *I* am Arthur Meade's right-hand man. Yes, sir! His right hand man," Bristol had a loose tongue when he was drunk.

"While you've been out on your cad... cattle drives," Bristol's drunkenness was impairing his speech. "*I've* been takin care of important business."

Revel spotted Collin Phelps moving toward them in the darkness of the alleyway.

"Hurry up," complained Crab from behind Revel. "We ain't got all night–"

"Shut up, Crab," yelled Bristol. "I'll do it when I'm finished enlightening Mr. Knox."

Revel continued to stand perfectly still. He smelled the wretched odor of Bristol's breath. He watched Phelps at the dark corner and listened to Crab moving his boots in the dirt behind him.

"Mr. Knox," Bristol pulled open the left side of his overcoat coat as he maintained his grip on the bottle of liquor in the same hand.

"You see this little notebook stickin' out of my pocket?"

"Yes," Revel replied with a perfect poker-face.

"Know what's in it?" Bristol smiled.

"The names and addresses of all your boyfriends?" Revel said with a smile.

Bristol struck Revel in the mouth with the butt of his Colt. "Don't get smart–"

"You want me to do it now, boss?" asked Crab from behind.

"No, no. It's alright, Mr. Crab," smiled Bristol as he pushed the barrel of his pistol to Revel's forehead.

"In this notebook, Mr. Knox, are the details of all of the murders that I've committed for our irreverent Arthur Meade," Bristol's voice grew loud as he continued to boast.

"Shut up, Bristol," blurted Crab from behind Revel, but Bristol ignored him.

"Oh, yes," continued Bristol. "Many murders. Dates, times, names, addresses, how I did 'em. Yes, you will show me respect before I kill you, Mr. Knox!"

"Shut up!" Crab's nervousness grew by the second.

"You shut up!" screamed Bristol. "The powerful Revel Knox is going to finally know that *I* am to be as respected as he is!" Bristol took another drink.

"Bristol," Revel interrupted in a low, controlled tone. "I have great respect for spineless drunks who beat women." Knox's eyes were intense and his words dripped of sarcasm.

Bristol's eyes narrowed as he stared at Revel. He was done with the conversation.

"Well, what you gonna do now, big brother?" Bristol asked as he pulled back the hammer of his long revolver.

Edward Crab grinned behind Revel. Intelligence wasn't Crab's strong suit.

"Listen carefully and I will tell you," Revel said in an eerily calm tone. "I am going to drop down, yank that smoke-wagon out of your hand, and kill you with it."

"That sounds like a good plan, but what you gonna do about Crab–"

Revel dropped to the ground causing Bristol to fire his pistol, but his drunkenness slowed his response time.

The bullet struck Crab in the center of his neck and Crab fell to the ground as blood squirted from his wound.

Revel, now in a squatted position, threw a hard punch to Bristol's genitals causing him to scream out in agony, falling forward toward Revel. Revel yanked the gun from Bristol's hand as Bristol fell forward toward him, simultaneously watching Collin Phelps positioned in the dark alleyway. Collin was drawing his weapon.

Revel spun the gun around, grabbed the handle and fired at Collin. The bullet went through Collin's right shoulder, causing Collin's arm to swing backward. He grabbed his injured shoulder and ran down the alley away from Revel toward the main thoroughfare.

Bristol Singleton, now on the ground, pulled his second pistol.

Revel quickly repositioned his aim toward Bristol.

"Don't do it, Bristol," Knox begged.

Bristol grinned as he slowly pulled the hammer back.

"Don't do it!" Knox shouted.

"I ain't got no choice," Bristol slurred his words as he lifted his gun toward Revel's head. Revel saw that the hammer of Bristol's gun was cocked and ready.

Revel fired a round into Bristol's stomach. Sorrow filled his heart. Revel dropped the gun and squatted down next to Bristol.

"Why did you have to–"

"Revel," Bristol whispered, interrupting Revel. "Didn't mean what I said about Elizabeth…" Those were his last words.

Revel pulled the notebook from Bristol's inner-coat pocket.

Gunfire rang out a few doors down. Collin Phelps had circled around the saloon and was now behind Revel.

Revel fled up the alley, away from the gunfire. He pulled his Cooper with his right hand while holding the notebook in his left.

"Revel Knox murdered Bristol Singleton!" shouted Phelps from behind the saloon.

Revel quickly untied Willow's reigns from the hitching post.

A flash from a muzzle and the sound of gunfire interrupted his thoughts. Phelps was now at the front corner of the saloon firing at Knox.

"*Move and live!*" Revel's mind screamed.

He shoved the notebook into his waistband, fired a shot in the direction of Phelps and mounted the horse.

Another shot from Phelps' gun filled Main Street.

Revel ducked instinctively. "Yah!" He yelled at Willow as he kicked her sides.

Revel slowed the Paint at the edge of his homestead. She walked in a slow gate until he stopped her in front of the barn.

He dismounted, lit a kerosene lamp, and quickly scanned the contents of the notebook.

"*This is unbelievable,*" Revel thought as he read the notebook.

The sound of hooves were coming toward the barn. Revel jumped back on Willow and bolted from the building.

"Elizabeth," he called her by name as she opened the back door.

"Revel! What is it?" Blood poured from his mouth and fear covered his face. Revel stepped into the rear foyer of her home and handed her Bristol's notebook.

He told her every detail about what had transpired during that evening. Revel then gave her a review of what was contained in the notebook that he had pulled from Bristol's pocket.

"Phelps was screaming that I had murdered Bristol!" he said to Elizabeth. She stroked his hair.

"Revel," Elizabeth interrupted. "Take deep breaths… slowly. Get control of yourself. We need to make a plan. I'll hide the notebook in our secret box."

Revel walked to her kitchen table and sat down at an end chair. Elizabeth sat down at the table next to him.

"Revel, you have got to leave Jefferson City tonight. We'll plan from this point… "

Chapter 37

[Thursday, October 15, 1877: present time]:

Singleton checked his watch. 11:35pm. He rolled a cigarette and leaned against the rear outer wall of Meade's law office… listening.

"Ms. Townsend," Arthur got her attention. "You must take it!"

"Mr. Meade, what are you doing?" She didn't understand.

"This is $10,000.00 cash. I want you to take it with graciousness," Arthur said as he shoved the cash toward her across the small table in the back room.

"You have served me for many years. You have, additionally, neglected your own family, your social life–"

"But, Mr. Meade," Ms. Townsend interrupted. "It's such a large amount. How long will you be gone?" She questioned as she looked at his gift on the table.

"A year at most," he replied. "This should be more than enough to satisfy you–"

"Mr. Meade, your money is not the basis of my loyalty to you–"

"I not only recognize this fact, but I am also extremely indebted to you, Ms. Townsend."

Jack flipped his cigarette onto the dirt of the alleyway and carefully peered through the bottom corner of Meade's rear office window. He had heard Meade and Townsend's entire conversation.

Jack saw the stack of cash on the table that Ms. Townsend was now picking up, then he spotted the bulky object under the small table… a huge bag of money.

"Ms. Townsend," Meade began. "I need a sabbatical from the practice of law, and the time away will do us both a tremendous amount of good. Don't you agree?" Meade spoke to Ms. Townsend while resting his chin on his clasped hands.

"Thank you, Mr. Meade," Ms. Townsend said humbly as she held the money in her hands. "Words cannot express my sincere appreciation."

Arthur smiled. "Thank you for accepting this gift, Ms. Townsend," Arthur said as he stood from the chair at the small table.

Ms. Townsend gathered her things and left his office. Arthur poured brandy into a short glass and took a drink. The terror of Jack Singleton being back in town made Arthur feel sick to his stomach, but the liquor numbed his senses. It gave him a feeling of confidence and strength.

Jack continued to watch him through the rear window, listening to every word.

Arthur looked down at the bag of money.

"$890,000.00!" Arthur said aloud. He began packing other bags in the small room at the rear of his office, talking out loud through his plan.

"The bank board is demanding a meeting with me in three days. Eula told me everything that happened at the bank with Singleton," Arthur said as he shoved files into his leather satchel.

"I'll leave day after tomorrow on the early morning coach." Arthur spoke through his plan, looking for any holes or problems. Arthur looked at the wall calendar to check the date of his planned departure: Saturday, October 17, 1877.

"I'll go home tonight. Avoid town tomorrow. Leave on the early coach the next day with the money. No law office, no wife, no Isabel, and no bank board!"

Meade sat back down as his mind went back to the evening of Bristol Singleton and Edward Crab's deaths…

Collin Phelps had appeared at Arthur's home late one night. Blood poured from his right shoulder while he talked rapidly to Meade. They sat at a backyard picnic table behind Meade's home under the light of the moon.

"And *Knox* has the notebook?" Arthur asked Phelps. "Are you *absolutely* sure?"

"Absolutely, sir. I shot at him when he was getting his horse, but don't think I hit him. He shoved the notebook into his pants and rode away. I Shot at him again but–"

"It's alright, Collin," Meade interrupted. "Thank you for coming here to give me this information in such an injured state. Can you make it to Dr. Bledig's?" asked Arthur.

Phelps stood from the table. "Yeah, I'll make it," replied Collin.

"Good man," Arthur said as he stood. "Your loyalty will be rewarded generously."

Arthur sat back down at his back-yard table and thought about his options.

"*Knox is on the run. I've got to get that notebook. Jack Singleton is too old. I'll pay the Director to put another man on Knox. Jack has been burned out and angry for months,*" Arthur scribbled his thoughts on a piece of paper.

"I'll meet with the US Marshal Director first thing tomorrow morning. I know who to suggest. I'll give him $500.00 to put his most 'unqualified' man on Knox, which will stoke Jack's anger. If this works, Jack will resign, and his resignation should open him up for private hire. He'll be gunning for Knox out of revenge for his brother's death and I'll fund his revenge." Arthur put down the fountain pen and lit a cigar.

"If that notebook gets into the wrong hands, it will be over… my money and my freedom. They'll hang me in the middle of town square." Fear filled Arthur's mind and heart.

"Yes, hiring Singleton to go after Knox will be the most effective and covert option."

Fear and worry of Jack Singleton and Revel Knox caused Meade mental and physical fatigue, but his focus was now on his money and escape… thoughts that gave him renewed vigor.

"Revel Knox and Jack Singleton, I'll have the last laugh!" Arthur shouted the words as he sat at the table.

Singleton, standing just outside of Meade's rear-office window, smiled as he turned toward the Drake Hotel.

"I could kill him right now and take the money, but Knox has got to be here somewhere. A little more time and I will kill both of them," he thought as he walked. *"Meade is leaving the day after tomorrow. Finding Knox is the primary objective."*

"Good evening, Mr. Knox," said the courteous hotel employee. Jack tipped his hat as he passed by the registration counter toward the staircase.

"$890,000.00 in that bag!" he thought as he climbed the stairs.

Jack entered his hotel room, locked the door, and leaned back against it. *"I'm forty-nine with few prospects,"* he thought to himself. *"$890,000.00 would make me a king!"*

Jack began to undress. His mind pictured what $890,000.00 would do for his future. He dreamed of building an elaborate ranch on the outskirts of Dodge City. His revenge turned toward greed.

"Kill them all: Knox, Meade, and Meade's wife. Take Arthur's bag of money," he thought as he removed his shirt.

Jack pulled off his pants and sat on the edge of the bed in a moment of motionlessness.

"That money would set me up for the rest of my life!" He continued his thoughts and smiled at this new dream.

He turned down the blanket and sheet and got into bed. The idea made sense.

"I can get that money!" he thought as he drifted into sleep.

Revel Knox bit off a plug of twist tobacco as he stood across the street from the Drake, staring at Jack

Singleton's dark hotel windows. Revel studied Jack's every move.

A well-dressed, heavy-set man scurried past him carrying a large bag. Revel instantly recognized Arthur Meade.

He counted Arthur's steps. When Revel's count reached one-hundred paces, he began to follow Meade.

Chapter 38

Jack woke early, packed his things, and checked out of the Drake Hotel.

He now sat at a table in one of Jefferson City's local diners eating a large breakfast: two eggs over easy, three sausage links, two pieces of buttered bread and strong black coffee.

He read the morning newspaper while sipping his coffee. *"Nothing in it,"* he thought as he laid the paper on the table and looked out through the restaurant's windows.

Jack scanned the boardwalk across the main thoroughfare. A large clock in Benning's Furniture Store read 6:15am.

He scanned further toward the left. A man caught his attention... it was that German businessman he'd ran into at the Old Dominion Bank.

As soon as Jack locked eyes with the man standing across the thoroughfare, the man turned away quickly and walked down the wooden sidewalk.

Jack jumped out of his chair, bolted toward the front door and ran into the street, scanning the crowd. The German had disappeared.

"Revel Knox," Jack said with an evil grin as he stood in the middle of the street. Wagons and riders passed him in both directions, yelling curse words demanding he get out of the street.

That *feeling* he had experienced at the bank now made perfect sense… that German businessman was Revel Knox!

"You owe for a meal, mister," a waitress hollered at Jack's back. She saw Jack run out the door and thought he was trying to "dine and dash."

He turned and walked back toward the restaurant's entrance. A foreign feeling filled Jack's body as he stepped over piles of manure in the street. It was a feeling of… fear.

"He's been following me, watching my movements. How could I have been so stupid?" thought Jack as he handed payment for his breakfast to an old woman behind the cash register.

Revel had seen Jack's eye contact, then turned toward the right and proceeded quickly down the wooden walkway filled with people.

Revel quickly lifted a hat from a sale rack on the boardwalk just outside of the front door of Jefferson City Clothiers, stuffed $5.00 into the hook on the hat-stand and put it on without slowing his pace.

After putting on the hat, Revel quickly pulled off his dark cattleman's jacket from his body and dropped it onto the boardwalk as he continued to walk briskly away from Singleton's position in the street.

Revel stepped left into the mud of the busy street toward a store that bore his family's name: Knox Dry Goods.

He looked casually back toward the restaurant as he walked. Jack Singleton stood in the middle of the busy thoroughfare with his Colt in his hand, scanning the crowd.

"*He recognized me,*" Revel realized. He watched as Jack holstered his gun and turned back toward the diner.

Chapter <u>39</u>

Singleton sat alone at the far rear corner of the saloon, smoking a cigarette and nursing a luke-warm cup of coffee. His table was dimly lit by a small candle.

He opened his pocket watch. 7:50pm. Jack put the opened watch on the table next to his ashtray.

"*Five more minutes,*" he calculated.

After seeing Revel from the restaurant during breakfast, Jack had spent the day patrolling the streets and alleyways of Jefferson City, but had no luck finding him.

Jack took another sip from his cup. He had been at the saloon since 7:00pm, rehearsing the plan in his mind.

After one last drag, he squashed the small remainder of the cigarette into the ashtray, closed his pocket watch, threw two bits onto the table, and stood to put on his riding coat.

"You're out of time, Mr. Meade," Jack said under his breath as he walked out of the saloon.

Jack reached to the inner pocket of the coat feeling for the envelope. It was still there.

"I'll leave this on Arthur Meade's dead body." The front of the envelope held the Drake Hotel's insignia and return address.

It contained Revel Knox's wanted poster – the poster Jack had pulled from the US Marshal's outer public notice board.

"They'll check the Drake and find Knox's name on the guest registry," Jack grinned at his own cleverness. It was a perfect way to frame Revel for the murder of Arthur and his Arthur's wife, Abigail. Two murders he would commit in the next hour.

"Knox will hang." The thought disappointed him over the lost opportunity to kill Revel with his own hands. However, capital punishment gave Jack a modicum of satisfaction. Framing Revel and reading of Knox's hanging would be a stalemate of reward for killing his brother, Bristol.

Jack left the saloon and walked toward Meade's home. Revel following, maintaining a safe distance behind.

Bristol's notebook was tucked inside Revel's jacket.

Chapter 40

Arthur and Abigail Meade argued in their large master bedroom.

"How many whores have you had?" she screamed at him.

"Your cold heart drove me to them," Arthur yelled in return as he packed his suitcase.

"So, you are *leaving* me?" she yelled the question through anger, betrayal, and tears.

"Abigail," he stopped his packing and turned toward her. "You and I have nothing more than a union of convenience," he said in the meanest of tones.

"Do you really think Isabel is anything more than a gold-digging whore?" Abigail asked as she lost complete control.

"At least she knows how to make me feel like a man," he barked back at Abigail and resumed his packing.

Abigail, an educated woman from an elite family on the east coast, ran toward Arthur in a fit of rage.

She pounded his chest with clinched fists. "I hate you! I hate you!" Abigail screamed through tears.

Arthur swung and punched Abigail in the side of her head, knocking her body into the closet door and onto the beautiful oak floor. Unconscious.

He continued to pack, concerned only with being on tomorrow's early morning coach.

Meade finished packing, picked up his suitcase along with the large leather duffle full of cash, and walked toward the bedroom door.

"Good riddance to you, Abigail," Arthur said as he stepped over Abigail's unconscious body.

Arthur walked quickly down the long dark hallway of his home toward the parlor. He froze when he saw the silhouette standing in the far corner.

"Hello, Mr. Meade," said Jack Singleton in the darkness.

Meade heard the unmistakable clicks of the Colt trigger being pulled into the cocked position.

"Jack, wait–"

Chapter 41

Arthur dropped his bags and held both hands in the air.

"Just wait a minute, Jack," Arthur pled. "We're both businessmen who want the same things: money and freedom."

"Mr. Meade," Singleton spoke in a calm and confident voice. "I want both of those things, but I want something else–"

"Anything!" Arthur interrupted.

"Shouldn't a good businessman desire to know what a second party desires before making an agreement?" Arthur's cowering disgusted Jack.

"Yes, certainly. What do you want?" Meade back-peddled.

"First, I'll take the $890,000.00 in that bag…"

Meade's eyes grew wider. "*How could he know the amount?*" Meade's mind raced.

"Secondly, freedom."

"Yes, certainly," Meade's eagerness increased Singleton's disgust.

"*Beg for your miserable life,*" Jack thought.

"And three, I want your heart roasting on a spit," Jack said flatly.

Arthur's slim hope begin to wither.

"Jack! I've been good to you!" Meade demanded, trying to show resolve.

"Samuel Underwood," Jack said with no emotion. Those two words removed all hope from Arthur's mind.

"Jack, please let me sit down before you kill me," Arthur asked humbly.

Jack waved his pistol toward the elegant Victorian chair at Arthur's left side. Arthur dropped into the chair and sighed audibly.

"Jack, you know me. You know my addiction for control and information. When you broke off communication with me, I had to find out if you were still alive. Underwood was simply a means to verify your movements–"

"That is a funny thing, Arthur," Jack interrupted. "Underwood said the same thing right before I put a bullet through the back of his skull."

Arthur clinched his teeth tightly as Jack verified what Arthur had suspected.

"Jack, make the smart decision. Let's split the money. We can both live the remainder of our lives as rich, free men."

"All of it, Arthur," Jack demanded.

"You know you can't get away with this–" Meade begged.

"Arthur," Jack interrupted. "Stop negotiating. I can and will get away with taking your blood money after I kill you." Jack pulled the envelope from his coat and flipped it onto the marble-topped coffee table.

Meade watched the envelope fall to the table's surface.

"What is that?" Meade's voice quivered.

"That, Mr. Meade, is a Drake Hotel envelope containing Revel's Knox's wanted poster."

"What good will that do–"

"When the Marshal finds this on your dead body," Jack interrupted, "He will go to the Drake and find that Revel Knox had checked into room 204, just last week.

"And when they find Knox, they'll prosecute him for your death, your wife's death, the murder of Edward Crab and most importantly, Bristol.

"He'll hang," Jack's words grew louder.

Revel Knox stood outside at the edge of the parlor window between the house and the evergreen bushes that lined Arthur Meade's home.

He tore through the bushes after hearing Jack's explanation of the envelope, reached the back door, and opened it quietly.

Revel pulled his Cooper and walked slowly through the dark house toward the direction of the parlor.

Revel stepped into the dark dining room. He could see Jack in the parlor.

Chapter 42

"Drop it, Jack," commanded Revel from the darkness of the Dining Room adjacent to the Parlor.

Jack instantly turned his gun toward the direction of Knox's voice. Meade bolted up from the chair, but didn't dare take a step.

"Revel, glad you could make it!" Jack said loudly through a smile. "Been a long time."

"*This is working better than I could have ever imagined,*" Jack thought as he held his pistol toward the darkness of the Dining Room. "*Kill 'em all here. Make Revel's death look like a suicide. Leave with the money!*"

"Jack," Revel called out to him, interrupting his thoughts.

"What?" Jack blurted.

"Jack, I'm going to holster my weapon and step into the Parlor so that you can see me. There are some things you need to know. Give me your word that you won't shoot until you hear me out," Revel said as calmly as possible.

"I give you my word, boy," Singleton lied.

Revel holstered his Cooper, raised both hands, and stepped slowly into the Parlor. The room was illuminated by moonlight from the Parlor's large plantation windows.

Jack could see something in Revel's hand.

"*Now I've got you,*" Singleton said in his mind as he started to squeeze the trigger.

"Bristol was killing people for Meade," Revel spoke quickly.

"You're a liar," growled Jack.

"Jack, it is completely true, and this," Revel said as he waved the notebook, "is Bristol's notebook. It is a diary of what Meade paid him to do. Just give me two minutes to tell you what your brother wrote," Revel asked with sincerity.

"Two minutes, Revel. It will be in your best interest to speak quickly," replied Singleton as he eased his finger off the trigger.

Revel described the contents of Bristol's notebook. He explained Meade's scheme and how Meade had hired Bristol to implement the brutal murders of the innocent German farmers.

Revel continued in telling what had really transpired during the night of Bristol and Edward's deaths.

"Time's up, Knox!" Jack stopped Revel.

The sound of the gunshot exploded through Meade's home. Jack Singleton's Colt .44 made a clunking sound as it hit the hardwood floor. Jack fell backward against the Parlor's wall and slumped to the floor. He had been gut-shot!

The explosion caused an instant recoil in Revel's body. He looked to the direction of the shot.

Arthur Meade held a small, double-barreled Derringer in his hand, which he was now pointing at Revel.

Arthur's excitement grew. He was back in control, and the realization that he would make it out of his house alive with the bag of money filled his heart with a calm supremacy.

Revel stood very still. He looked at the small weapon in Arthur's hand. Revel's plan had failed. His life was about to end.

"Revel, it's a shame you found that notebook," said Meade as he pulled the trigger back in preparation to fire the second round. "I've known you and your family for a long time."

Meade gently squeezed the Derringer's trigger. Another explosion filled the house. The bullet entered one side of his head and exited the other.

Chapter 43

Arthur Meade died instantly. His body collapsed over the wing-back chair and bounced onto an expensive rug covering the oak floor.

Revel caught himself as he fell backward against a dining-table chair. He was staring toward the opening of the hallway at smoke drifting from the end of a postol.

Abigail Meade's hands shook violently as she began to weep. She dropped the gun and fell to her knees.

Revel rushed to her side. Abigail rolled into a fetal position on the floor at the opening of the hallway.

"Shh, shh, it's alright, Abigail." Knox pulled her into his lap, then brought her head to his shoulder.

She wept and moaned.

"Revel, I've killed him," she wailed. "I've killed him!"

"Abigail, you did what had to be done, and you've saved my life in the process." Revel said softly into her ear.

"I'm so sorry for what he has done to you, Revel. I had no idea–"

"Abigail," Revel interrupted. "We're going to collect your things and I am going to take you to Elizabeth's," he said as he helped her to her feet.

"It's over for me, Revel," she managed to say as she continued to weep.

"Arthur drained our bank accounts. He has cheated on me so many times, and he hit me–"

"Abigail," Revel interrupted again. "You have done nothing wrong–"

"I should not have shot him, but when I was listening to your words from the hall, and when he was about to shoot you–"

"Stop it, Abigail," Revel said firmly. "We don't have much time. Get a bag and pack only what is necessary. Do you understand me?"

"Yes," Abigail replied as she steeled herself for the task of packing.

Revel's legs trembled from the adrenaline as he stopped his Appaloosa at the edge of Abigail's front steps. He reached down to her, took her by the arm and lifted her up into his saddle. She wrapped her arms around him, then he kicked his horse toward Elizabeth's home.

Chapter 44

A few hours later, the Marshal and his deputies looked through Meade's luxurious home. Old Dominion Bank officials, residents of Jefferson City, and newspaper people filled Meade's front lawn.

"What do we got?" asked the young deputy just arriving on the scene.

The Marshal struck a match and held the flame over the bowl of his freshly packed pipe.

"Two things for certain. Envelope on the coffee table is from the Drake Hotel," said the Marshal as he watched the crowd on the lawn.

"What's in it?" asked the deputy.

"Wanted poster… for Revel Knox," the Marshal said as he turned to look at the deputy.

"Knox? "I'll be –"

"Second," interrupted the Marshal. "Two bleeders."

"Two?" The deputy was as confused as the marshal.

"Go on in," encouraged the Marshal through puffs from his pipe. "See for yourself."

The deputy entered the large foyer and turned into the Parlor. He scanned the room. Blood spatter covered the walls.

"Over here," an older deputy called out. He walked over to Meade's body and squatted down next to his associate for a closer look.

"Killed himself?" asked the younger as he looked at the gun in Meade's left hand. It was a .44 caliber Colt with a wood-grain handle… Jack Singleton's pistol.

"Nah, don't think so," said the older. "Look at that over there," he pointed. The younger followed the direction of his associate's finger and saw the large pool of blood in the parlor's corner.

"Whose is that?" Asked the younger.

"*That's* the question, young man," the Marshal spoke from the opening of the Parlor. He puffed on his pipe and stared at the blood.

"And," the Marshal continued, "look at the trail… goes through the house and out the back door."

"You think it's got anything to do with those rumors about Meade's problems with the bank?" asked the deputy.

"Gotta be connected somehow," replied the Marshal after pulling the pipe from his mouth. "He was definitely getting ready to head out."

"How do we know that?" asked the young deputy.

"His bag is packed with clothes over by the big chair," the Marshal motioned with his pipe.

"Think the wife killed him?" asked the deputy.

"Abigail?" the Marshal laughed. "That woman wouldn't hurt a fly."

"Where's she at?" asked the older deputy from his squatted position at Meade's body.

"Can't find 'er," the Marshal admitted.

"Boys," the Marshal said to his deputies as he turned toward the front door. "Check with the neighbors. See if you can find any witnesses."

"Marshal?" The older deputy got his attention as he walked toward him. "Found this inside Meade's coat pocket."

The Marshall took the notebook and scanned the contents.

The Marshal looked up at his men with wild eyes. "Find the wife, find Singleton and find Revel Knox!"

Chapter 45

"Marshal," said the young deputy. "Got a minute?"

The Marshal sat his pipe into the custom made lazy Susan at the corner of his desk.

"We've finished interviewing Martha Poste. She works as a prostitute at the Vineyard Saloon–"

"I know who she is," interrupted the Marshal. "Get on with it."

"Well," the deputy continued, "Claims she witnessed Revel's fight with Bristol, Crab, and Collins, from her second story window at the saloon about six months ago."

"Knox *was* telling the truth," stated the Marshal.

"Yep," said the deputy with a smile.

"Good work, Ben," replied the Marshal. "So, Bristol's notebook, along with Poste's story, will clear Mr. Knox. Any word on his location?"

"Not yet, sir, but we're working on it."

"What about Meade's wife?" the Marshal asked.

"Can't locate her, either sir," the deputy replied with a hint of shame. "She's vanished. You think Singleton took her?"

"Don't worry 'bout it, Ben. We'll find her," replied the Marshal. "What about Jack Singleton?" he asked.

"Listen to this, Marshal. Shelton Boyd just reported that someone stole a horse from his barn early this morning while it was still dark!" Ben said with excitement.

"You're kidding me?" the Marshal stood from his chair.

No, sir! Boyd just finished giving a sworn statement that he saw the thief emerge from his barn with one of their horses. He also confirmed that one of their saddles and some supplies had been stolen, as well."

"Boyd owns a big ranch and several barns," said the Marshal as he thought out loud. "Did he get a shot off?" asked the Marshal.

"Yeah, Marshal. Said he fired three times with that new Evans repeater rifle of his, but didn't think he hit him," Ben replied.

"Son, I've known Shelton for a long time and I know he can knock the wings off a grasshopper at a hundred paces–"

"But, Marshal," interrupted Ben. "The thief was riding one of Boyd's Campolina studs."

"Ah – makes sense. I wouldn't want a bullet near a horse like that, either," the Marshal admitted.

"Did Boyd see the guy?" asked the Marshal.

"That's what I was gettin' to, Marshal. Boyd said it could have been Singleton, but he wasn't sure. Said the thief was clean shaven. Didn't have Jack's mustache, but he did find blood in his barn," said the Deputy.

"Get Boyd to come to the office, and get Scherbaum over here to meet with Boyd. We'll see if

Scherbaum can draw up a sketch of the guy that Boyd saw," the Marchal instructed and Ben turned to leave.

"Hang on, Ben," the Marshal stopped him. "Have Scherbaum make two drawings. Have him sketch out the description given by Boyd, then have him do a second drawing with a handle-bar mustache. We'll dispatch the drawings to the Calvary posts in the surrounding states."

"Yes, sir," said the deputy with a quick exit.

The Marshall pulled his pipe from the lazy Susan, struck a match and lit the bowl…

"Singleton is alive and on the run," mused the Marshal. "Where's Meade's wife? And where is Revel Knox?"

Chapter 46

Millie read a Bible story to sixteen children gathered around the campfire. The sun had almost disappeared over the western horizon.

"Jesus said, 'Father, forgive them for they know not what they do,'" Millie read aloud.

Movement on the eastern horizon caught her attention.

"Children, go home quickly," she said as she turned toward their small group. The children ran away from the fire toward their respective tents.

Two Shawnokwan men stepped to Millie's side, rifles in hand.

The man coming toward their camp drove a small wagon, pulled by two horses. He wore a large-brimmed hat and traveled at a slow pace.

The wagon stopped next to Millie.

"Millie?" said the driver.

Several Shawnokwan men gathered around the wagon, with some looking at the contents in the rear. It was filled with food, various supplies, a couple of rifles, and… a large leather duffle bag.

The men were shocked at what laid in the forward left corner of the wagon… two items: a Shawnokwan blanket and a hand-made Shawnokwan skinning knife.

The wagon driver pulled off the large hat and long blonde hair fell to her shoulders.

"My name is Abigail Meade. Revel Knox said you could help me…"

ORDERING INFORMATION

This book is always on sale directly from the author at:

https://www.michaelshankministries.com

You can also order from Amazon.com, Kindle, Barnes & Noble, Books-a-Million, Ingram Books, The Book Depository, the Apple Store, and over 60 online book retailers.

OTHER PUBLICATIONS

Muscle and a Shovel

Muscle and a Shovel eBook

When Shovels Break (sequel to Muscle and a Shovel)

When Shovels Break eBook

Muscle and a Shovel 13-Week Student Workbook

Muscle and a Shovel 13-Week Teacher's Manual

Muscle and a Shovel Spanish Version

Muscle and a Shovel Portuguese Version